J. T. EDSON'S
FLOATING OUTFIT

The toughest bunch of Rebels that ever lost a war, they fought for the South, and then for Texas, as the legendary Floating Outfit of "Ole Devil" Hardin's O.D. Connected ranch.

MARK COUNTER was the best-dressed man in the West: always dressed fit-to-kill. THE YSABEL KID was Comanche fast and Texas tough. And the most famous of them all was DUSTY FOG, the ex-cavalryman known as the Rio Hondo Gun Wizard.

J. T. Edson has captured all the excitement and adventure of the raw frontier in this magnificent Western series. Turn the page for a complete list of Berkley Floating Outfit titles.

J. T. EDSON'S
FLOATING OUTFIT
WESTERN ADVENTURES
FROM BERKLEY

J.T. Edson

TERROR VALLEY

BERKLEY BOOKS, NEW YORK

Originally printed in Great Britain by
Brown Watson Limited.

This Berkley book contains the complete
text of the original edition.
It has been completely reset in a typeface
designed for easy reading and was printed
from new film.

TERROR VALLEY

A Berkley Book / published by arrangement with
Transworld Publishers Ltd.

PRINTING HISTORY
Corgi edition published 1968
Berkley edition / March 1984
Third printing / February 1987

ISBN: 0-425-09569-X

A BERKLEY BOOK ® TM 757,375
Berkley Books are published by The Berkley Publishing Group,
200 Madison Avenue, New York, New York 10016.
The name "BERKLEY" and the stylized "B" with design
are trademarks belonging to Berkley Publishing Corporation.
PRINTED IN THE UNITED STATES OF AMERICA

CHAPTER ONE

A Cougar as Big as a Burro

Few if any of the crowd in the Silvertip Saloon paid any attention to the drumming hooves of a horse approaching rapidly along the main street of Robertstown, New Mexico. Any cowhand who found himself delayed while coming into town, to spend in a night most of the wages received for a month's hard work, tended to try and make up the lost time. However, the leathery old timer who burst through the saloon's batwing doors showed more than the usual eagerness to reach the bar. Crossing the room hurriedly, he halted close by where the bartender served a couple of customers.

"Gimme a drink, *pronto*, dammit!" he ordered. Then he turned to the two men on his side of the bar, breathing lustily in their direction. "Can ye smell any likker on her?" he demanded, eyes glinting a mite wildly and normally expressionless face showing more expression than the bartender could ever remember seeing.

If either of the customers took exception to the old timer's action, they did not show it. Sniffing the air like a redbone hound searching for a coon's line, the taller of the pair finally shook his head.

"Can't say as I can."

"You're sure?" asked the old timer, ignoring the

brinkfull glass of whiskey slid his way by the bartender.

"Lon's got a nose like a bluetick trail hound, friend," drawled the smaller man. "Looks a mite the same way, too."

"Which last part's a lie, Dusty," stated the taller man and then went on to reassure the old timer further. "Happen there was anything to smell, I'd smell it."

Apparently the proof of the old cowhand's sobriety disturbed him. Shoving back his hat, he ran a hand through his thatch of white hair.

"Then I saw it!" he groaned, scooping up the glass and tossing the whiskey down his throat in a single gulp. "Let's have another one, Bo."

The two young men turned back to the bar and reached for their beer glasses. Before they could do more than sip at the cold, golden brown liquid, the old man brought his attention back to them. Eyeing them in a distrait manner, he shook his head and rat-holed the second drink offered by the bartender.

"If I wasn't drunk, I saw it," he told them, darting wild glances about the room as if in search of corroboration for his words. "Which same I'd rather be drunk and not've seen it."

Then the full impact of what he had done struck him. Any man who went around deliberately breathing into strangers' faces, no matter how well intentioned his motives, asked for trouble in sizeable chunks. He studied his barside neighbors with interest, and not a little concern.

Maybe some folks, especially if not reared in the West, would have thought that the old timer had little to fear from either man's objections to his actions. Having been born and raised in cattle country, old Gaff Whittaker could read the signs and go beyond the externals to see what lay beneath. His scrutiny of the two young men told him that he might count himself lucky that they did not protest at his undue familiarity.

On the surface, the taller man stood maybe six foot in height and with a lean wiry frame. Man might be an exaggeration, for his handsome, almost babyishly innocent features made him look no more than sixteen at most. Tanned Indian-dark, the face appeared young, almost naive—until one noticed those red-hazel eyes. Being a shrewd observer, when not under stress, Gaff saw the eyes first. Reading the cold, latent savagery in the eyes, he did not regard the face as young; it might be in years, but not in practical experience. The young man wore range clothes, yet did not strike Gaff as being a cowhand. Fact being, he did not give signs of following any specific trade. Every item of clothing from hat to boots, including the gunbelt, was black. Butt forward at his right side, hung a walnut-handled Colt Dragoon revolver, balanced by an ivory-handled James Black bowie knife at his left. To be wearing one of the old over-heavy Dragoon revolvers in the mid 1870's usually pointed to lack of enterprise in being unable to purchase a more modern weapon. Everything about the Indian-dark young man told Gaff that did not apply in his case. While the young man might appear innocent and inexperienced on the surface, Gaff saw through the exterior and knew that he had been very fortunate that the other did not take offense at being breathed on.

The second man hardly rated a second glance, taken on externals. Like his companion, he wore Texas style cowhand clothing of good quality. However he gave the impression that the clothes must be cast-offs—yet they fitted him well enough to have been made for him. Some folks might have seen no more than a small, insignificant Texas cowhand, but not Gaff. He saw dusty blond hair beneath the pushed-back, expensive J. B. Stetson hat; a tanned, handsome face that had strength of will, intelligence, power of command and a sense of humor etched on it. That was a man's face—a *big* man's face at that. Under the cowhand clothes was a powerful frame, happen one looked careful, hinting at strength beyond the mere five foot six of height. Around the Texan's waist hung a well-made gunbelt, matched white handled Colt Civilian Model Peacemakers riding butt forward in fast-draw holsters. If the wearer could use that gunbelt to its full potential, Gaff figured himself to be more than lucky the Texan did not object to having breath puffed into his face.

"Say, I'm right sorry, gents," Gaff apologized. "I shouldn't have come up like I did."

"You'd likely got real good reason for doing it," said the small man, his voice an easy, lazy Texas drawl.

"You might say that," Gaff agreed fervently, "after what I saw—Or what I hope I didn't see."

"Sounds kinda scarey," grinned the dark youngster, looking even younger than ever. "It's a good thing that Mark's not here yet, Dusty. He'd like to pee his pants all night if this gent's been seeing ha'nts.''*

"It warn't ha'nts I saw!" protested Gaff. "Fact being, I ain't certain sure I saw nothing, drunk or sober."

"You got me all interested, Gaff," the bartender put in. "Tell us what you saw so's we can decide whether you saw it or not."

Knowing the old timer, the bartender felt considerably surprised. Normally Gaff was the most laconic and unemotional of men, having over the years faced every disaster and calamity to plague a cowhand. Stampedes, drought, storm, flood, rangefire had all assailed him at one time or another without causing him more than a momentary concern. Only an incident of unprecedented magnitude could make the old timer act so perturbed.

If it came to a point, way things stood in Roberts County, only something of a most serious nature would bring Gaff into town on this particular evening. Before

*Ha'nts: Haunts, Texas name for ghosts

the bartender could continue with his last line of thought and realize its full implications, Gaff spoke again.

"You sure you want to hear about it?"

"If it's something fit to tell afore clean-living visitors to our fair city," assented the bartender and grinned to show the Texans—notoriously touchy when out of their home State—that he meant no offense.

"Go right ahead," agreed the small man called Dusty. "I can always hold Lon's hand while we walk back to the hotel happen it's too scarey."

"Bet you would anyways," put in a voice from along the bar.

Slowly the Texans turned their heads to look at the speaker. A bunch of cowhands gathered in the background and had been listening to the conversation. While four of the six seemed bent only on enjoying pay-day, the other two spelled trouble; or the Texans had never seen it. Both were tall, well built and dressed in cheap versions of the latest cowhand fashion. Sullenly handsome, the speaker had a cocky self-assurance and truculence in his bearing; and possessed a local reputation as a hard-case and something of a bully. The second had much the same reputation, without attempting to surpass his companion.

"Leave off, Wally," said one of the bunch. "You know what the boss said."

"I forgot the Rafter Bar was in," grunted Gaff and turned his attention back to the Texans as if he had said all that needed saying in the matter.

"You was going to tell us what you saw, or didn't see," the bartender went on hurriedly, for he too had read the two Texans' potential correctly and wanted no trouble in his place. "Reckon these gents are like me, want to hear about it."

"Reckon we do," drawled Dusty, swinging around to put his back to the Rafter Bar hands.

"Tell ahead," drawled Lon, resting his elbows on the bar top and standing so he could watch the cowhands' actions reflected in the bar mirror.

The two hard-cases seemed to be taking notice of their companion's warning, for they swung back to the bar and resumed their drinking. However silence dropped over the group and, without giving a sign of it, they clearly listened to the conversation of Gaff's party.

"You know anything about cougars?" asked Gaff soberly.

"They've got four legs sticking down, one to a corner, at the bottom; a long tail and claws," Lon described profoundly.

"Look sort of like a house-cat only different," further explained his companion, sensing that they might be victims of some local joke.

"Ever seen one?" asked Gaff.

"A house cat?" asked Dusty.

"Naw! A cougar."

"Well now, I reckon I can say 'yes' to that."

"A big 'n'?"

"He was a *Texas* cougar, friend," Lon said. "They don't come no bigger than that."

Along the bar, Wally Bratley, the handsome hard-case, let out a disbelieving snort of laughter; but he stood fast. Like the bartender, he knew Gaff and wondered that the old timer would come to town on a night when sure to find the Rafter Bar crew present in force.

"You got cougar in Texas as big as a burro?" inquired Gaff.

"Now me," Dusty replied cautiously, still suspecting a joke, "I'd say that depends on how big a burro you had in mind."

"I've seen some mighty small burros and some real big 'n's," Lon went on.

"Look, gents," groaned Gaff. "I'm needing advice."

"Which same you couldn't've come to a worse place to get it, if I do say so myself," drawled Lon.

"What's up, friend?" asked Dusty, but his attitude had changed slightly.

Watching the old timer, Dusty felt less certain that they might be in the process of being set up for some local joke tried on newcomers as a prelude to stinging them for a round of drinks. He read a deeper concern on Gaff's face than could have been put there by acting.

"It happened this way," Gaff said, sensing a sympathetic ear. "I was riding our west line not far out of town. Well, I comes out on top of a rim and down below there's a small bunch of cattle grazing. I figured on going to look them over and chase any strays back off our graze——" He threw a defiant glare at the Rafter Bar men, but they made no comment so he continued. "There's a steep bank near the cattle and all of a sudden this damned great cougar jumps off it, lands on a cow and bowls her over——"

"How big're the cows up this way?" interrupted Lon, still thinking it might be a joke of some kind.

"Don't start that again," ordered Dusty.

Strange as it might seem, that dangerous-looking Indian-dark young man did not appear to object to the small, insignificant cowhand addressing him in a commanding manner; although Lon did not seem to be the kind to accept orders easily.

For all his acceptance of his companion's order, Lon felt puzzled. Despite his apparent lack of years, Lon knew a thing or two about mountain lions. Even an exceptionally large Texas cougar only rarely topped the two hundred pound mark and the Sierra Madre variety of puma found in New Mexico was smaller still. True even the Sierra Madre cougar possessed fine killing equipment, but it lacked the size and weight to knock a full-grown range steer off its feet when springing down from a bank.

"Best tell us about it," the dark youngster drawled. "Have a drink first."

"Not just now thanks," Gaff answered, "but you can mark it up for me, Bo."

"I'll do that," the bartender replied, his curiosity aroused by the story. The sight of a cougar making its kill should not have so much effect on the hard-bitten old timer. "What happened then?"

"Well, I tell you, I just sat my hoss there and stared. I've never seen a cougar that big afore. Anyways, I figures that a .44/40 bullet ought to chill its milk a mite and reaches for my Winchester. Then dog-my-cats if that cougar doesn't lay hold of the cow's neck and start to haul it off towards the cut-bank wall."

"I've heard that a cougar'll drag off its kill," Dusty commented.

"Sure," agreed Gaff. "A pronghorn, or a whitetail deer. But this was a full-growed range cow that'd been well-fed."

"Must have been a tolerable strong cougar," drawled Lon, still unsure whether he might be falling for a hoary old local joke.

"You haven't heard it all yet," Gaff stated.

"There's more?" smiled Dusty.

"That's what I'm not sure about," admitted Gaff.

"Why not tell us and see if we're sure?" Lon inquired.

"Anyways, I got to figuring that a cougar that big'nd strong'd be better off as a rug on the bunkhouse floor. So I get out my rifle and gets set to take him when he stops by the wall. Which same I didn't go for taking him on the move. Only he doesn't stop there. Now that cut-bank's maybe twelve foot high and, so-help-me-Joe, that there cat jumped clear up it with the cow on its back."

Silence followed the words. Dusty threw a glance at the bartender, but saw no sign that he expected such an end to the story.

"He took the cow up that bank with him?" asked Lon,

"That's just what he did," agreed Gaff. "Which, afore you tell me, is damned impossible. Only I saw it happen. That cougar seemed to slide itself under the cow and then jumped. Clawed a mite on top and hauled it and the cow plumb over."

Once again silence greeted the end of Gaff's words. If the story should be a joke, it fell mighty flat. Yet the two Texans could not see how the story was anything other than a joke as they analyzed the words. While a cougar could easily leap up a twelve-foot, and higher, cut-bank, taking the carcass of a full grown cow up at the same time seemed mighty improbable to say the least.

"You don't want to believe a word he says, do you, Laslo?" warned Bratley, turning from his companions.

"Sure don't," agreed the second hard-case. "Them Bradded Box bunch see things all the time."

"Things that don't exist," Bratley went on.

"Such as?" bristled Gaff.

"Such as the Bradded Box being on beef they butcher, even when it's not there at all."

"You saying that we've been slow-elking Bratley?" growled Gaff.

While a bully and trouble-causer, Bratley possessed a fair streak of caution. His boss gave certain orders before the ranch crew came into town and Tom Brinded did not speak idly. So Bratley wanted it to appear that Gaff started any trouble that might come about. Only by making the Bradded Box man appear the aggressor could he be sure of his party's support. He had never seen the Texans around with the Bradded Box crew, but they might be newly hired; or, even if strangers, could side up with Gaff in the event of a fight.

"Naw, I'm not saying that," he answered. "Maybe that big cougar's been taking our stock."

"And maybe it took young Billy Winson when he was

riding your line," Laslo continued, glaring at Gaff. "Or grabbed off Wart Geary."

"Yeah?" spat out Gaff. "And what about Fritz Dieter from our spread. He took out one morning and never come back."

"Likely he couldn't take working for a rat-hole outfit like the Bradded Box no more," suggested Bratley.

"Or it could be that he saw something he shouldn't and got left for wolf-bait," Gaff snarled, pride in his outfit overriding his caution.

At that moment Gaff realized that, being so perturbed at what he saw on the range, he made the mistake of coming to town on the night that the Rafter Bar crew received their pay. At one time all the local ranches paid out on the same day and their crews swarmed into Robertstown for a celebration. Recently events changed the state of peaceable, friendly rivalry between the spreads, suspicion ran rife and bad trouble hovered ever in the background. To avert trouble, the town marshal called in the ranch owners and demanded that they paid out on different days, the remaining crews staying clear of Robertstown and allowing the cowhands of the spread which gave out the wages a clear run.

Such had been the shock Gaff received that he forgot the ruling and headed for town as being nearer than his ranch. He had wanted confirmation that he had not imagined the incident, or have it caused by consumption of whiskey in a hurry. Instead it looked like he had found trouble. Bratley and Laslo would not let his grey hair or advancing years prevent them from jumping him as a member of a rival outfit. Being a stubborn cuss, with his fair quota of loyalty to his brand, Gaff refused to even consider the possibility of flight to avoid trouble.

"Take it easy, Brat," the bartender put in. "We don't want any fuss."

"And won't have any," promised Bratley, failing to

sound sincere. "I just thought this pair of drifters didn't know what sort of company they're keeping."

"It's been all right up to now," Dusty said quietly.

"And what's that mean?" demanded Bratley.

"Try figuring it out for yourself," drawled the small Texan.

Possessing something of a reputation for salty toughness around Robertstown, Bratley had become used to receiving more deference than the short-grown newcomer showed him. Most men, including several of more imposing appearance than the Texan, watched how they spoke and acted in Bratley's presence; the more so when he stood backed by Laslo and with four more of the Rafter Bar crew in the close vicinity.

"You pair are maybe working for the Bradded Box?" Bratley asked, knowing an affirmative answer would unite his party against the Texans should it become necessary.

"Can't say that we are," Dusty replied.

"Way I remember it," Lon continued. "I work for Dusty here and he never said as how we'd changed bosses."

"We haven't, Lon," Dusty said. "If that answers this *hombre's* question."

"All right, so you don't work hereabouts," Bratley growled. "So when I tell you, friendly-like, you're in bad company, I allow that you ought to be friendly and get out of it."

"Way I see it, *hombre*," Dusty told the bulky cowhand. "*You* forced the company on to us."

"Which same, happen you look down," drawled Lon, eyeing Bratley sardonically, "you can see the answer to it."

"Huh?" grunted Bratley, glancing at the floor. Seeing his feet he caught the dark youngster's point. "Why you——"

At which point he became painfully aware of a

change in the two Texans. No longer did they lounge at
the bar. Or rather although they still lounged, there was
a subtle difference in the way they did it; a relaxed
readiness that gave a warning to anyone smart enough
to read the signs. Bratley could read and understand
what he saw. He did not like it.

"Looks like the Bradded Box's took to hiring its
fighting done," he said.

"That'd be their way," Laslo agreed, eyeing the small
Texan's gunbelt. "They reckon we won't stack against
hired guns."

"And they reckon right," Bratley went on, starting to
turn away from the two Texans as if backing down.

All in all it was a creditable performance and one
which, when used before, lulled an intended victim into
a sense of false security. Only one thing spoiled the play.
On the last occasion Bratley acted in such a manner,
Gaff had been present and saw what followed.

"Look out, Texas!" the old timer yelled and lunged
forward.

Pivoting around in a continuation of his turn, Bratley
hurled a blow at the small Texan's head and caught
Gaff full in the mouth as the old timer came between
them.

CHAPTER TWO

I've Enough Troubles
Without You Two

In accordance with their usual practice at such times, Laslo had moved around so as to put their prospective victim between them. He made the move while Bratley spoke in such a casual-appearing manner that one might have forgiven the small Texan for failing to notice the danger.

Even as the old timer shot aside under the propelling force of Bratley's blow, Dusty lunged forward. He closed with Bratley before the other recovered from the surprise of Gaff's action and ripped a left fist solidly into the big cowhand's belly. Breath whoofed out of Bratley's lungs and he felt a similar sensation to once when the cook's chuckwagon mule kicked him in the stomach. Jackknifing over, he went back a couple of paces.

Laslo acted without thinking, following the routine he and Bratley perfected for such an occasion. Jumping forward, his big hands reached out ready to lay hold of the Texan when Bratley's fist struck home. Unfortunately for the plan, Bratley failed to do his part—and it seemed that Dusty did not fail to notice Laslo's movements.

Bending forward and twisting his body so that Laslo's

hands missed him, Dusty balanced on one leg, driving the other in a kick to his second attacker's solar plexus. Letting out a croak, Laslo folded over. Like a flash Dusty turned to face the man, catching him by the right wrist and shoulder. Then, with a surging heave, Dusty turned and hurled Laslo forward, full into Bratley. Up rose the small Texan's right foot, placing its sole against Laslo's rump and shoving hard. Already off balance, the two men reeled backwards and went down in a tangle.

Seeing the pride of the Rafter Bar—using the term loosely, for in more peaceable days the two men's trouble-causing had been an embarrassment rather than an asset—go down, the rest the party began to move forward. Lon thrust himself from the bar, blocking their way. Legs apart, hand turned palm outwards, fingers slightly crooked ready to close on the walnut handle of the old Dragoon, the tall young Texan stood exuding a deadly menace. No longer did his face look young and innocent. Now it held the cold, slit-eyed savagery of a scalp-hunting Indian.

"I promised my mammy I'd never do no fist-fighting," he warned the Rafter Bar boys, his voice the deep-throated grunt of a Comanche Dog Soldier. "Which same I don't reckon on breaking my word. Likewise you're staying out of it, too." Although Lon did not mention an alternative to his suggestion, the cowhands knew of one. Should they take cards, it must be with guns and on a permanent basis; that Indian-dark Texan's attitude made it plain. While all the four local hands wore guns, they did not class themselves as gunfighters. Given a chance, they would have cut in with their bare hands to avenge their ranch's honor. Lon stopped that chance and the quartet hesitated before taking the ultimate step of gunplay. In the days before the mysterious disappearance mentioned by Bratley and Gaff the Rafter Bar hands spent many a merry evening with the Bradded Box's crew. So far the trouble between the ranches had not come to anything more than name calling and mean-mouthing. The four young men did not wish to take it to shooting.

Snarling with rage, Bratley rolled the winded Laslo from him and lurched to his feet. His eyes came to rest on the small Texan and he let out a bellow of rage, lowered his head and charged at the other in a rush that ought to flatten him like a stomped-on flap-jack.

Even as Bratley reached him, Dusty fell backwards. The bigger man's hands missed and he felt the Texan grip his shirt then ram a foot into his mid-section. Just what happened next Bratley could never quite figure out. He felt himself falling forward, his head going down while the foot in his middle thrust his body upwards. The room seemed to spin around before Bratley's eyes, then he crashed down flat on his back upon the floor. Although used to falling, Bratley had no chance to lessen the impact and his landing jarred breath and cohesive thought from his head.

Dusty rolled on to his shoulders after flipping Bratley through the air and bounced to his feet ready to meet Laslo. However the second man showed caution—or acted in a real stupid manner, depending on how one looked at it. Having seen what happened to Bratley, Laslo discarded his original idea of launching a fist attack on the Texan. Instead he reached for his gun and Gaff saved his life. Whipping up a chair, Gaff smashed it across Laslo's shoulders. Wood splintered and the man shot forward. Dusty met the uncontrolled rush, his left fist driving across to meet the man's jaw with a solid click. Instead of being shot, as might have happened had he drawn his gun, Laslo pitched sideways and crashed to the floor.

At that moment the batwing doors opened and Tom Brinded, owner of the Rafter Bar, entered. Taking one glance at the situation, the tall, burly rancher reached for the Colt holstered at his side.

In a move so fast that the eye could barely follow it, Dusty's right hand crossed his body to draw the Colt from his left holster. Steel rasped on leather, merging with the click as the Colt's hammer rode back under the Texan's thumb even as the four and threequarter inch barrel of the Peacemaker cleared the holster. Yet even at such speed the Texan's forefinger did not enter the triggerguard, nor the gun reach full cock, until the barrel lined away from him. Many men found difficulty halting their gun in the desired position when using the cross draw, but the Colt stopped moving and rocksteady, ready for use.

Brinded froze, fingers still not touching the butt of his gun and eyes glued on the barrel of the Texan's Colt as it aimed at his favorite belly. A cold, sick anger bit into Tom Brinded. It seemed that Dale Vivian of the Bradded Box had so far forgotten their old friendship as to import hired guns. If that blond cuss let his Colt's hammer fall, no jury would convict him as he drew in what would pass as self-defense.

"You this pair of yaboos' boss?" asked Dusty.

"Sure," Brinded replied, his voice brittle.

"Then call 'em, and the others, off afore somebody gets hurt real bad."

Considering that Bratley lay writhing and groaning in a heart-rending manner, while Laslo sprawled on the floor with his body jerking mindlessly, Brinded wondered how much worse the Texan regarded as real bad. However the rancher stood still and made no hostile moves. Such lightning fast drawing of a gun was the exception rather than the rule and a man did not take time to perfect it unless he also burned enough powder to be able place his bullets where they would do most good once the draw ended. Being unable to do anything, Brinded sensibly did it. He realised that the Texan could have shot him and did not, so doubted if a bullet would come unless he gave cause for it.

"Are you pair hired for the Bradded Box?" he growled, then saw Gaff's face.

Blood ran from the old timer's mouth corner and Brinded could guess at who caused it. However he owed his men something in return for the loyalty they gave him and wanted to avoid facing the unpalatable fact that most like Bratley or Laslo began the trouble. His question to the small Texan was in the nature of an excuse for his own crew's actions.

"Like we tried to explain to your hired men," Dusty replied, "we're not working for anybody hereabouts."

"Then why'd you jump my boys?"

Some folks might have called that a mighty peculiar question, comparing Dusty against the size and bulk of the two Rafter Bar cowhands; but in some strange way he seemed to have put on height and heft until he gave the impression of being the biggest man in the room. Certainly Brinded did not consider his question incongruous when faced with the evidence that met his eyes on entering the saloon.

"There's some'd say your boys jumped me," Dusty countered and his Colt returned to leather with the same flickering speed.

Which, as Brinded well knew, meant that nothing had changed. Sure the Colt had been replaced in its holster, but it could easily be fetched out again; and if the need arose, Brinded doubted if it would remain unfired a second time. Before the rancher could decide on his next course of action, the matter was taken from his hands completely.

Stepping cautiously, Town Marshal Garve Green entered the room. With the instinctive second sense gained wearing a law badge in more than one town, Green had headed for his office the moment he received word of Gaff's arrival in the Silvertip Saloon. After collecting a ten-gauge, twin-barrelled pacifier from the rack on his office wall, the marshal headed for the saloon. From what he saw while approaching the bat-wing doors, the shotgun and his presence might be necessary.

"Look like there's been some fuss," Green commented.

"I kept my boys out of town when the Bradded Box paid off last week," Brinded pointed out, determined to support his crew and keep them out of trouble.

"How about that, Gaff?" asked the marshal, more relaxed than any of the local men expected and showing a remarkable ease in the presence of the two efficient-looking Texans.

"Well, now, I reckon I'd good enough reason for coming in tonight," the old timer answered.

Bratley had recovered sufficiently to sit up. Glaring wildly around, his eyes took in the man who handled him with such devastating ease, then went to where his gun, tipped from its holster during his unexpected somersault, lay on the floor. Out shot his hand, but a boot came into his line of vision and kicked the revolver away before he could touch it. Turning angry eyes to the intruder, Bratley looked up at Marshal Green's coldly contemptuous gaze.

"Don't be *loco* all your born days, Bratley," the lawman ordered. "Happen you don't know it, that's Dusty Fog."

Behind the bar, Bo let out a low grunt which mingled with the soft-spoken surprise expressed by others of the crowd as they heard the name. Ever since the two Texans started talking with Gaff, the bartender tried to guess at their identity and failed due to his inability to reconcile the small Texan's appearance with all he heard of the man called Dusty Fog.

Somehow one did not expect a man who had been the youngest and, many said, the most able cavalry captain in the War Between the States, and was now segundo of

the biggest ranch in Texas, a master cowhand, trail boss
and town-taming law enforcement officer of the first
water, to be of such small insignificant appearance.

Yet Dusty Fog was all of that. During the War he commanded Troop "C" of the Texas Light Cavalry and
carved himself a name equal to that of Turner Ashby
and John Singleton Mosby at the peak of Dixie's hard-
riding, raiding horse-soldiers. With the end of the War,
Dusty returned to his home and started to help rebuild
the great OD Connected ranch. Force of circumstances
made him a trail boss—Texas beef could only be sold by
taking it on foot to the railroad in Kansas—and peace
officer, but he built himself a name as one of the best in
both lines. His speed on the draw and deadly accuracy
caused many to call him the fastest gun in Texas. From
his uncle's Japanese servant, Dusty had learned the
fighting arts known as ju jitsu and karate and put them
to use in off-setting his lack of inches when handling
bigger men in bare hand combat.

Such then was the man Bratley picked on when he
tried to jump the small Texan and Marshal Green gave
real good advice when he prevented the other picking up
the gun.

In halting at the second Texan's order, the remainder
of Bratley's party had showed considerable good sense.
Knowing the small Texan's identity precluded any need
for further introductions. Where Dusty Fog was, there
one could usually find two more men; one of them, lean
as a steer fed on greasewood, tanned Indian-dark and
clad all in black, went by the name of the Ysabel Kid.

There was good reason for the Kid looking and
sounding like a Comanche when riled. His father had
been a wild Irish-Kentuckian adopted by the supreme
horse-Indian tribe of the Texas plains and who married
the daughter of Chief Long Walker's French Creole
squaw. Out of the mingling of fighting bloods came a
son. Initiated into the dread Dog Soldier lodge, Loncey

Dalton Ysabel learned all its deadly and effective fighting, raiding and scouting techniques. He could move in silence through the thickest bush, follow a trail where most men could see nothing to guide them, handle his bowie knife like an extension of his arm and turn his Winchester rifle into a super extension of his will. Although not *real* fast with his old Dragoon Colt—it took him all of a second—twice as long as needed by Dusty Fog, draw and shoot—he could still have made the quartet regret disobeying his request.

While Bo cursed his stupidity in not identifying the two Texans sooner, he excused himself with the thought that Dusty Fog did not look how one expected a man with his reputation to be, and the Kid had only been referred to as "Lon"; while the third member of Ole Devil Hardin's floating outfit, Mark Counter, was missing.

Although Gaff felt highly pleased at being backed by such distinguished patronage, he recalled with a slight shudder how he acted on his arrival. Before he could think more on the matter, the old timer saw Green's eyes studying him then turn to the bar.

"How about it, Bo?" asked the marshal.

The question put Bo in something of a spot. Being a businessman who relied on cowhand trade for a major proportion of his livelihood, he had no wish to antagonize either Brinded or the Bradded Box. Yet whichever way he answered the marshal, he would offend one party.

"Hell, twarn't nothing but a misunderstanding," Gaff put in.

A state of feud might exist between the two ranches, but Gaff had been raised to believe such things must be forgotten in the face of a common danger. He knew that Green would take a severe line to prevent trouble breaking out in Robertstown; up to and including jailing, or slapping a real heavy fine, on the participants as a warn-

ing and deterrent to others. While the old timer did not
care for Bratley or Laslo, and possessed a fat lip as a
memento of the former's fist, they were still cowhands
and should be kept out of the law's hands.

"I'd admire to hear about it," drawled Green sardonically.

"You wouldn't believe Laslo there done swooned
away on account of the heat?" asked Gaff.

"Nope."

"Or how Bratley slipped on a pile of buffler fat?"

"There ain't no buffalo fat on my floor," Bo pointed
out indignantly.

"Which same, I'm still wanting to know what happened." Green warned.

"Well, there's a reasonable explanation someplace,"
Gaff said, scratching his head. "Trouble being I'm
damned if I can think of it."

"Why not mark it down to cowhand fooling,
Garve?" asked Dusty. "I don't reckon there's any real
harm done."

Seeing a chance to escape without loss of face,
Brinded nodded. "I'll go along with that, Cap'n Fog.
How about it, Wally?"

Muttering something under his breath, Bratley
lurched to his feet. However he knew that none of the
others would side him against their boss' orders and so
gave a surly agreement. Swinging on his heel, he walked
to where Laslo lay sprawled and groaning back to con-
sciousness. The remainder of the Rafter Bar party
gathered around to help raise Laslo and tote him to a
table.

"You done whatever you wanted to do, Gaff?" asked
Green meaningly.

"Reckon so," the old timer replied.

"Best get back to the Bradded Box then."

"How about telling us where you saw that cougar?"
Dusty put in.

"I'd sure admire to see one that big," the Kid agreed.

"Cougar?" Green put in.

"That's what brought me into town," Gaff explained. "I'll tell you about it over a beer."

"Not here," Green answered. "Down at the office."

The marshal felt curious as he made his reply. Since coming to Robertstown, he had seen enough of Gaff to know the old timer was no trouble-causer who would head for town hunting fuss with a rival outfit. Nor was Gaff a boozehound, sneaking into town when he should be working on the range. The reference to a cougar also aroused the marshal's interest, for he loved to listen to hounds making their music as they followed a mountain lion's trail. He could not imagine why a cougar would bring Gaff into town instead of heading to the ranch.

"I reckon we'll come along," Dusty put in.

"Was going to ask you," Green replied, knowing that the continued presence of the two Texans in the saloon might provoke further trouble. Bratley had a vindictive nature and would not soon forget the licking taken at Dusty's hands; liquor could give him the necessary false-courage to make a play against the Rio Hondo gun wizard.

Buying four bottles of beer, Gaff led the way from the saloon. At the Rafter Bar's table, Bratley threw a look of hate after the departing Texans and tried to explain his actions to a sceptical Brinded. The rancher declined to discuss the matter and repeated his warning to avoid trouble with the Bradded Box; range wars were ruinous things and Brinded wished to avoid one if possible.

"If the Bradded Box's hired them two Texans——," Bratley began.

"Which we know it hasn't," interrupted Brinded. "You forget Cap'n Fog, Wally. The OD Connected's one spread I want no part of."

Giving a low sniff that could mean anything, Bratley resumed his drinking. The fact that Brinded and the remainder of the crew, with the exception of Laslo, settled down to enjoy pay night in the traditional fashion did nothing to lessen Bratley's desire for revenge.

At the marshal's office, open beer bottle in his hand, Gaff told his story for the second time. At its end, he took a long pull at the beer and then looked at the other three.

"Well?" he asked.

"Damned if I know," confessed the marshal. "Happen you'd taken enough likker to make you imagine it, you'd be too drunk to sit a hoss."

"Which same you was sober when you hit the Silvertip," the Kid went on with a grin. "Even if you didn't act it."

"I don't usually go 'round breathing into strangers' faces."

"That figures," said the Kid dryly. "Happen you did, you'd never have lived to get all old and ornery. How about it, Dusty, did he dream it up?"

"I don't know, and that's for sure," Dusty replied. "A man can dream some mighty strange things sometimes."

Even as he spoke, Dusty thought back to a dream—or had it been reality—that haunted him, dating from a time when he rode alone down trail from the Kansas railhead to Bent's Ford in Oklahoma.*

"It seems a mite hard to believe," Green commented.

"It's *damned* hard to believe," Gaff corrected. "A cougar knocking down and killing a full-growed cow's bad enough. But when it hauls the cow off *and* jumps up a cut-bank with the critter on its back——."

Words failed Gaff and he took another pull at his beer. None of the others could offer the old timer any

*Told in THE FAST GUN by J. T. Edson.

consolation or advice, so he took his departure after finishing the beer.

"I'd sure like to see a cougar that big," drawled the Kid after Gaff left the office.

"Happen Mark's not come in before, we'll take us a look tomorrow," Dusty answered, for Gaff had given them a good description of where he saw the incident.

"Are you staying around here, Dusty?" Green inquired.

"That depends on how soon Mark arrives. He ought to have beaten us here, but he's not come."

"Where's young Waco and Doc Leroy?" asked Green.

"The boy took lead over to Backsight and Doc stayed on with him.† Lon and I waited until he was over the worse and then headed back."

"That'd please Waco," grinned the marshal, knowing the close ties which held Ole Devil's floating outfit.

"We couldn't do anything else and he'll likely join up with us later," Dusty answered. "Anyways, if Mark's not in, we'll go and take a look for that cougar."

"If it's big enough to do what Gaff reckoned," drawled the Kid. "It shouldn't be roaming around an itty-bitty *county* like New Mexico."

"*County!*" yelped Green, pride in his home State plain in his voice. "Anyways, Texas ain't so big."

"That depends," Dusty smiled.

"On what?" demanded Green.

"Whether you count Texas as a country, or just a State. You didn't sound any too happy to see us, Garve."

"I'll tell you the truth, Dusty," the marshal said frankly. "I'm not." He looked at the two men and went on in explanation, "I've enough troubles without you two being here."

† Told in RETURN TO BACKSIGHT.

CHAPTER THREE

I've Changed My Mind About You

Knowing that Marshal Garve Green had been his father's friend and also owed the members of the floating outfit something of a debt of gratitude, Dusty felt puzzled at the other's words. Nothing showed on the Kid's face, but his attitude clearly indicated that such a statement was what he expected from a lawman —the Kid could never forget that he had once been a border smuggler who caused various peace officers considerable trouble and had a fair piece of it given back by them.

"Sounds bad," drawled Dusty. "What sort of trouble've you got, Garve?"

"Just about the worse kind," replied Green. "That fuss down at the Silvertip might have blown Roberts County wide apart. I tell you, Dusty, this whole section's likely to explode and blow apart at the seams any day now."

"How come?"

"There's been a fair amount of slow-elking going on. In fact more than a fair amount. There's been a hell of a lot of it."

"Slow-elking's bad," Dusty admitted.

"There's more than that," Green warned. "At least

six men have disappeared."

"How'd you mean, disappeared?" the Kid asked.

"Just that, Lon. Take young Billy Winson of the Rafter Bar. He left their place to hunt for strays and didn't come back. Brinded's crew went out looking for him and couldn't find a trace. Well, they didn't think too much about it at first. Bratley and Laslo had been hounding Winson and making his life miserable, so Brinded figured he'd most likely hauled his freight. Only thing being that he'd left all his thirty-year-gatherings* behind."

"Which doesn't look like he'd left of his own free will," Dusty commented.

"He hadn't much, few clothes, stuff like that, nothing personal," Green answered. "And Bratley can be real mean when he's riled."

"So *you* figured Winson had left the area," Dusty said.

"I'm town marshal, it happened on the range and out of my jurisdiction," Green pointed out. "Anyways, Joe Vasquez's deputy sheriff up this end and he looked into it. Joe reckons that Winson was afork a real good horse and might've figured it worth more than a few cheap clothes—or did figure it until Wart Geary disappeared about two weeks after Winson took off. This time Brinded really searched. He cut that range like it was spring round-up. Didn't find Geary, but learned that somebody had been slow-elking in a big way."

"How big?" asked Dusty.

"They looked to have been hitting at least once a week for months, taking half-a-dozen head at a time. Killed, butchered and loaded on to a wagon, the hides buried on the spot."

A low whistle left Dusty's lips, although it was not

*Thirty-Year-Gatherings: Cowhand's personal belongings no matter what his age.

caused by hearing the hides had been left behind. That
could be expected; one piece of meat looked like
another, but the hide invariably carried a brand on it by
which ownership might be easily established. What
caused Dusty's whistle was the number of head taken.
As segundo of a ranch, he knew the value of cattle and
estimated what the slow-elking must have cost Brinded.

He also knew the dangers of such a situation and
understood Green's concern about his and the Kid's
presence in Roberts County. Slow-elking, illegally killing and butchering cattle, ranked with cow stealing in
the ranch owner and cowhands' opinion; being regarded
as crimes for which death offered the only sufficient
punishment. While a traveller might be excused killing
one head if really hungry and unable to shoot some wild
animal, taking a whole bunch could not be overlooked.
The full implications of the affair went beyond the
ranch dweller's objection to being robbed, for Green
implied that the culprit had not yet been discovered.

"Why didn't somebody start following tracks?"
asked the Kid, making what, to him, appeared the obvious solution.

"Joe Vasquez did, and he reckons to be pretty good
at following sign," answered the marshal. "Trouble
being that he needs sign afore he can follow it. Only
both times there'd been heavy rain between the feller
disappearing and a search started. It washed out any
tracks."

"So then either that Bratley jasper, or some other
hothead started talking and laying the blame on some
other outfit," Dusty guessed.

"Which's just how it happened," agreed the marshal.
"Bratley started giving it out that Bradded Box knew
where the stuff went. Nobody took any notice at first.
Of course all the other ranchers started combing their
range and they found that somebody had been making

big antelope in fair numbers every damned which ways."

"All of them?" asked Dusty.

"Every one brought in hides as proof. Then first one spread and another started to lose men. Naturally they'd got hands riding the range pretty frequent and four more have disappeared, every time without a trace. You know this's a tolerably damp section——?"

"They do say you get your share of rain, and more," Dusty answered.

"It rains good and regular, that's for sure," said Green. "The gang only hit when rain clouds gather over the Wapiti Hills and the rain washed out all their sign."

"You said all the spreads had been hit and lost men," drawled Dusty. "Surely that points to some outside bunch."

"That's what I've used to keep the ranchers from painting for war," Green replied. "It might've worked, only you know cowhands."

"I've met a few," admitted Dusty dryly. "Some of them tend to jump the easiest way, especially trouble-makers like Bratley."

"He started saying that whichever ranch did the slow-elking, it'd make it look like they were getting hit too —which I admit makes good sense to me" Green said. "Not that I'd want to admit it aloud."

Dusty could imagine how the situation developed. At first the various ranch crews would work in harmony to try to discover their common enemy. Then, as time passed without success, discontent and anger at the loss of companions rose. Under those conditions a few idle words might easily lead to real bad trouble. It said much for Garve Green's ability as a lawman that nothing more serious than talk came up over the months since the first disappearance.

"It's not been easy to hold things down," Green admitted when the small Texan congratulated him on his success. "There was a fight between the Lazy V and DM boys last pay day that might've blown things wide apart, but Joe and I managed to cool it down without gunplay. I knew that by this month things wouldn't be so easy. So I called in all the ranchers and asked them to spread their paying out, make sure that only one spread had men in at a time."

"It looks like they agreed," commented the Kid.

"They did. None of them wants a range war any more than I do."

"That figures," Dusty said. "They've too much to lose by it."

"I've got the town held down," Green went on. "But what scares me is that it might blow up on the range."

"Sure," Dusty agreed. "If men from two of the outfits meet out there, a wrong word could set it off."

All too well Dusty knew the tempestuous nature of cowhands and their intense loyalty to the brand hired them. Once a cowhand tossed his bedroll into a ranch's wagon—even if only figuratively—he became a part of the outfit and fully committed to any action it took. A chance meeting on the range, with feelings running so high, and old friendships would be forgotten. Every man wore a gun for his protection; one killing might easily spark off a range war that would ruin every rancher in the county.

That, in a way, accounted for Green's lack of cordiality at seeing two good friends. While never seeking trouble, Dusty bore the reputation of being real fast with his guns. Such a reputation attracted trouble like iron filings to a magnet. A young hard-case wishing to make a name for himself often sought out one of the top guns with the intention of forcing a fight and gaining fame by emerging victorious. If that happened in Roberts County—with the usual result of a dead or badly wounded aspirant to fame—the remainder of his crew were likely to say Dusty worked for some other outfit, with the inevitable demands for revenge.

Although the Kid did not have the glamor of being a top gun, he might also have a fight forced on him. His Indian-dark, innocent face and choice of armament often led trouble-causers to make the mistake of picking upon him, with fatal, or near-fatal, results. If that happened under the present conditions, an ugly situation might easily develop.

The fact that Dusty and the Kid sided with Gaff, a member of the Bradded Box, would not go unnoticed and might be construed as support for that ranch. So any incident involving a hand from one of the county's other ranches could easily flare up into the war Green dreaded.

"I'll steer clear of trouble," Dusty promised. "But I fixed with Mark to meet him here and aim to do it."

"Just who do you reckon's behind this slow-elking, Garve?" asked the Kid.

"There you have me, Lon. I've known all the local ranchers and businessmen for around three years and don't see any of them being mixed in a thing like it."

"Would any of them be needing money?" Dusty wanted to know.

"Not that I know about. The cattle business's good and most of them are clear with the bank, or getting that way."

"How about in the neighboring counties?"

"We've the San Mig Apache reservation on two sides, Dusty. Azul Rio County's to the south and the Wapiti Hills to the west."

"You can forget the Apaches," drawled the Kid. "They wouldn't take the time or trouble to butcher any beef they stole."

"And there's only three spreads in Azul Rio," Dusty went on. "I know all the owners, they're honest and you can trust them."

"Which leaves the Wapiti Hills," the Kid finished.

"Do you know them?" asked Green.

"We know about them," Dusty replied. "Enough to swing around them any time we've come through this way."

"I'm tolerable surprised you white folks didn't try to give 'em to the Injun brother," said the Kid sardonically. "Seeing's how they're just about rock and nothing else. Make a real good reservation, I'd say."

If you're getting bitter, we'd best have you fed," Dusty told his friend, although he had to admit there was something in the Kid's views on what the white man regarded as an ideal home for Indians.

"I feel a mite hungry myself," Green went on. "We'll go along to the hotel and see what they can do for it."

Any further discussion on the slow-elking had to be postponed until after the meal. On arrival at the hotel, Green and the Texans were joined by a couple of local businessmen and the talk turned to general subjects rather than county problems. One of the men owned a store and gave out a bit of news which interested both the Texans. It seemed that he had taken over a nearly new Conestoga wagon and team in security for a sizeable loan and became owner when the other party died in a mining accident. Having no use for the big wagon, the storekeeper offered it to the highest bidder. A freight outfit bought the wagon and promised to send along a driver to collect it.

"Should be here by now," the man complained. "Maybe Killem's changed his mind and don't want it. That'd just be my luck."

"Did you say 'Killem', Happy?" Dusty asked, having been introduced to the storekeeper. "Would that be Dobe Killem?"

"Sure."

"I wonder——," Dusty said.

"I hope not," the Kid went on. "If Mark met her, he might be days afore he gets here."

"Met who?" Green inquired, although he could guess from what he knew of the Killem freight outfit.

Before either of the Texans could enlighten the marshal, Happy—so called because of his pessimistic outlook—continued with his tale of woe. To listen to him, everything he touched went wrong. He felt sure that even if Killem intended to honor their agreement, either the driver would get lost or become involved in a disaster during the trip to Robertstown.

"Happen he sends old Calam along," said the Kid consolingly, "the disaster'll not start until after she gets here."

"And if Mark's stopped off fooling around with her, I know who'll be in the middle of it," Dusty stated.

Happy refused to be consoled. After a tirade of woe and misfortune which had befallen him, or which he fondly expected to happen momentarily, he sat back and gave a long sigh.

"Way I look at," he said. "You die if you worry, you die if you don't—might just as well have the pleasure of worrying."

Despite Happy's predictions that the food would fail to arrive due to accident or illness among the hotel staff, or doubts as to whether it would be eatable, all the party enjoyed a good meal. Avoiding the two businessmen's attempts to continue the evening at the Silvertip, Green, Dusty and the Kid returned to the jail.

"You don't reckon the slow-elkers could be hiding out in the Wapiti Hills, Garve?" asked Dusty, resuming their interrupted discussion.

"I don't," the Kid put in. "There's nothing but rock walls and gorges——"

"Somebody don't reckon so, Lon," remarked the marshal.

"Not even outlaws'd hide out there if they had two choices," the Kid said.

"There's a feller called Count Giovanni got him a place up in the hills," Green told the Texans.

"What's he raise bighorn sheep?" drawled the Kid.

"I don't know as how he raises anything," Green answered. "Been in there for maybe six months now. On his way out, he telegraphed the county sheriff and me to meet up with him here. When he arrived, he told us that some Italian secret society had put the Injun-sign on him and was after his scalp, so he aimed to move into that Spanish mission that's in the Wapitis. We knew it was there, but nobody's ever bothered to go in and look it over."

"Why'd he tell you all that?" Dusty inquired.

"Wanted to get things clear right from the start. He doesn't intend to have anybody poking around his place. I tell you, Dusty, he sounded one scared *hombre*. He allowed that the Mafia, or whatever he called them, had put the death sign on him and that he daren't trust any strangers to come near him, them not being above hiring a killing if they can't do it themselves."

"That could be cover for something else," the Kid pointed out.

"Which's why he wanted to see the sheriff and me, us being the nearest law to him. The Wapitis lie across the county line, but the sheriff they come under's on the far side of them and doesn't worry much about visiting them. Anyway this Count jasper had a letter from the Department of the Interior, the Italian Ambassador, and the Governor of New Mexico——"

"Sounds tolerable popular," drawled the Kid.

"Sure," agreed Green. "He insisted that we telegraphed them all, at his expense, to check they were for real. Which they were. All of them asked that we gave him every cooperation."

"And just what co-operation did he want?" asked Dusty.

"Only that we made sure everybody in the county stayed away from his place. No social calls, visits, anything."

"How'd he figure to live in the Wapitis?"

"Allowed that according to the old mission records there's a fertile valley maybe a mile wide and three long around the buildings. It's got grass, water, trees."

"That's not much, happen he aimed to set up ranching."

"Which he doesn't," Green told the Texans. "There'd not be enough land to run cattle, although it'd support his remuda happen he didn't have too many hosses."

"How's he fixing to live then?" Dusty said. "Is he in there alone?"

"Took his wife, maybe ten, fifteen men and gals along when he went in."

"Then how's he feed them?" Dusty demanded.

"Buys his supplies here in town," the marshal replied.

"What sort of men were they he took in?"

"Real mean-looking cusses, eyes colder'n a diamondback rattler's. Allowed they were his bodyguard. Now me, I'd rather not have them guarding my body."

"Do they give you any trouble?" asked the Kid. "When they come into town, I mean."

"None of 'em's ever been in, not the way you mean. Once every couple of weeks they come in with a wagon, couple of 'em riding guard on it and a driver, collect supplies and go back the same day. They've never been in the saloon, or anywhere but the general store."

"Do you know how much stuff he buys?" Dusty queried.

"I checked on that," Green replied. "It's enough, including the meat, to feed all the bunch he took in."

"Have you thought of going in to see him?"

"Like I said, Dusty, he told us right out that he didn't

want anybody going in there. Few folks went along at first, but there's only one way in, through a narrow neck, and there's always four men with rifles covering it. They just wouldn't let anybody through at all."

"You're the law, Garve," the Kid reminded.

"Town marshal," corrected Green. "And you know that my jurisdiction ends with the city limits."

"Why not call on the county sheriff over the line?" asked Dusty.

"For what?" countered Green. "Don't forget those letters he brought. There's a powerful heap of weight behind him. We'd need more than just suspicion to push in there."

"You could be right," drawled Dusty. "I——"

"There's somebody coming in fast," the Kid remarked, crossing the room and looking from one of the windows facing Main Street.

Joining the Kid at the window, Green gazed at the approaching rider. "It's Joe Vasquez!"

Bringing his horse to a halt before the sheriff's office, the tall, slim rider dismounted. He did no more that toss his reins across the hitching rail before bounding on to the sidewalk and making for the office door. Dressed in ordinary range clothes and wearing a low-hanging Artillery Model Peacemaker, only Vasquez's olive-hued skin and dark eyes gave a hint of his Latin birth. Certainly his accent carried no trace of his Spanish blood.

"We've got trouble coming, Garve," he announced on entering. "I was over to the Bradded Box and everybody there's all riled up because old Gaff's not come back from riding the line."

"He's all right," Green answered. "We saw him off just a couple of hours back——"

"And his hoss came in all lathered to a muck-sweat, wall-eyed with fear and toting an empty saddle," the deputy sheriff interrupted.

"So what's happening?" demanded Green.

"Dale Vivian's got all his crew together and they're coming into town to find out what's happened to him. As soon as I saw the way things were going, I grabbed my horse and headed for town, figured to warn you."

Before the marshal could ask any of the questions which formed, he heard the distant, but rapidly approaching drumming of a number of horses' hooves. From the amount of sound, the marshal estimated that Vivian must be bringing in all eight of his crew. By that time, the Rafter Bar ought to be carrying enough liquor to make them ready take up any challenge. Unless the situation was handled with care, the trouble the marshal sought to avoid might blow up. His eyes went to the two Texans and he found them watching him with an interested gaze.

"I've changed my mind about you pair," he told them. "Fact being I'm right pleased to see you here."

"Which same, coming from a lawman, means he wants us to do something that could get us killed," drawled the Kid.

"I wonder what that could be," Dusty went on, and held out his hand. "All right, Garve, hand over the deputy's badge."

CHAPTER FOUR

Captain Fog Acts Persuasive

Listening to the sound of the approaching Bradded Box crew, Dusty estimated that he and the local law had time to make a few quick arrangements. He knew better than to rush blindly into a dangerous situation. If the time to plan offered itself a wise man took it.

"How d'you want to handle it, Garve?" he asked, pinning the deputy's badge on to his calf-skin vest. "You know these fellers and I don't."

"Reckon we ought to block off the street, stop them reaching the Silvertip?" asked Vasquez.

"If I know Dale Vivian, he'll call in here first," Green answered.

"Then I'd say let him come to us," Dusty put in. "He'll do that if he wants to avoid trouble."

"Dale's a mite hot-tempered, but he soon cools down too," the marshal said. "We'll play it your way, Dusty."

For all that, the few seconds that it took for the Bradded Box crew to reach the marshal's office seemed to spread out over a considerable length of time. Green remained seated at his desk and tried to act nonchalant, but worry gnawed at him. If Vivian did not act as they planned, he and his men might reach the Silvertip before the law could halt them. The consequences then could be disastrous.

The hooves came to a halt outside. Glancing around his office, Green read a hint of relief on his three companions' faces.

"Wait out here, al of you!" snapped an authoritative voice and leather creaked as a man dismounted.

On entering, Dale Vivian threw a glance around the room. Green sat behind the desk with Vasquez by his side. At the left of the room, the Kid stood feeding bullets into the breech of one of the office rifles. To the right, Dusty held a shotgun broken open for cleaning—or loading. The rancher proved to be a tall, slim, tanned man in his late thirties. Tough, capable with neither arrogance nor bluster in his manner was how Dusty summed him up. A good man for a friend, but a tolerable bad enemy. Such a man needed firm, but careful, handling.

"I reckon you know why we're here, Garve," the rancher said, throwing another glance at Vasquez.

"Do I?" Green countered.

"Joe lit out to tell you we were coming. Old Gaff's gone now."

"Joe told me."

"What do you aim to do about it?"

"Me?"

"Don't fuss me, Garve," Vivian growled. "You know Gaff was in town tonight; and we both know the Rafter Bar's here."

"So?" asked Green.

"I said don't fuss me——!" barked Vivian.

"We saw Gaff in town," admitted the marshal. "And we saw him leave. He left here without trouble."

"And he didn't get home. His hoss came in, but he wasn't on it."

"So Joe told me."

"Then what're you sitting resting your butt end in here for?" demanded the rancher. "Why aren't you hauling Brinded's bunch down here?"

"On what charge?" asked Green.

"Damn it to hell——!" Vivian shouted.

"We've been friends for a fair time, Dale," Green interrupted. "But I won't stand for even a friend coming in here shouting orders at me."

"All right, marshal," Vivian answered in a lower tone. "Happen you don't see your way to doing your duty, I'll take my boys down there——"

"You'll take them to the hotel and hold them there," Green put in. "I'll go down to the Silvertip and ask if any of the Rafter Bar crew've left since Gaff rode out."

"Maybe I will—or maybe me and the boys'll go to the Silvertip for a drink."

At which point Dusty made his presence felt in no uncertain manner. With a twist of his wrists, he closed the shotgun's breech, giving out a solid clang in the silence following the rancher's words. Vivian had been in such a hurry to start the wheels of justice turning that he overlooked the two Texans. At the clang, his eyes swung in Dusty's direction. Back East a shotgun might be regarded as a sporting device designed to hurl a cloud of small balls at a fast flying bobwhite quail, but not anywhere west of the Mississippi. To folks on the western ranges, a shotgun was a weapon, a mighty effective one under certain conditions. In the hands of a trained peace officer, it became a hell of a fine inducement to keep the peace.

And, mister, that *big* blond *Tejano* was a trained peace officer; or Dale Vivian had never seen one.

"They do say the liquor's just as good at the hotel, mister," Dusty said quietly. "That's where you're going."

"You'd best listen to him with both ears," the Kid

warned, having completed the loading of the rifle and feeding a round into the chamber with a smooth flick of wrist and loading lever.

Vivian stiffened slightly. While a fighting man from shoulder to hock, he was also capable of thought. Maybe Joe Vasquez, born and raised in Roberts County, or Garve Green, a good friend and poker playing associate, would hesitate to push their orders to the limit; but that did not apply to the two strangers from Texas.

"How'd you know that Gaff came in?" Green asked.

"There was a bottle of beer in his saddle pouch," the rancher explained, wanting time to think and pleased to be given it.

"He came in all right, bought the beer and left," the marshal said. "Now, if you're ready to act sensible, Dale, I'll do my part."

Before the rancher could make any reply, the office door opened and two cowhands entered. While both sported lowhanging Colts, they did not have the look of professional fighting men hired for weapon-skill alone. However Dusty knew their type all too well. Brave, they had still to learn prudence and obedience to the law. To them, a peace officer was somebody paid by town folks to stop cowhands having fun; or, as in the present instance, prevent them doing what they regarded as right.

"I told you to stop outside," Vivian growled.

"Got to figuring you might need help, boss," said the taller hand.

"Looks like you do," agreed his companion.

"Tell them, Dale," Green ordered.

"Go down to the hotel," said the rancher.

"Rafter Bar's at the Silvertip," the taller cowhand pointed out.

"You heard me, Lee."

"Happen the john laws're making you say it, boss, me and Jack's got a right good argument for 'em," the taller youngster announced.

"You said it, L——," Jack agreed.

"Here!" barked Dusty, and tossed the shotgun across the room.

Seeing the nine pound or so of steel and wood flying at him, Lee forgot his first intention and grabbed upwards to catch the shotgun. His companion's mouth still hung open from when Dusty interrupted him and eyes bugged out in amazement; as well they might. On releasing the shotgun, Dusty's hands crossed and the matched Colts left their holsters. Even before Lee caught the shotgun, Dusty's revolvers lined on him and his companion.

So swiftly did it happen that even Green, who had seen Dusty in action and knew his chain-lightning speed, was taken by surprise. Vivian and his two men just stood and stared, unable to think of making any move against the Texan's control of the situation.

Then a glint crept into Lee's eyes as he realised that he held a mighty convincing argument in his hands. Slowly his fingers coiled around the wrist of the shotgun's butt and forefinger entered the triggerguard.

"Don't be *loco*," Dusty warned. "It's not loaded and mine is."

"Put it back on the rack, Lee," Green ordered.

"Do like the marshal says!" growled Vivian.

"Hey, boss!" called a voice from outside. "Couple of Rafter Bars're coming out of the Silvertip."

"Lon!" said Dusty, for his friend stood by the side door nearest to the saloon.

Without waiting for any further orders or instructions, the Kid left the room. Maybe Green, as town marshal, should have made the decision of what to do, but he left it in Dusty's capable hands.

"Maybe they're coming looking for trouble," Vivian growled.

"You'd best go hold down your crew then," Dusty replied, holstering his guns.

While Dusty made the move as a gesture to show the
rancher that he trusted him, Lee regarded it as an ideal
opportunity to break the law's hold over them. Moving
forward to obey his boss' order, he suddenly lunged and
swung the shotgun's butt around, then up in the direction of the small Texan's head. The rancher opened his
mouth to yell a warning recognising the danger to his
foolhardy young hand and expecting to see Lee go down
with a bullet in his belly.

In that the rancher underestimated Dusty. All too
well the small Texan knew that a shot from inside the
office would be all the waiting cowhands needed to
hear. So, even had he meant to use his Colts, he could
not without provoking the very thing he wanted to
avoid.

Stepping back a pace, Dusty avoided the blow. His
hands shot out in smoothly coordinated moves, the
right catching the twin barrels from underneath while
his left hand clamped down on the breech just over
where Lee's fingers curled around the small of the butt.
Feeling Dusty's pressure, Lee used his strength to try to
twist the gun back again. That was what Dusty wanted
the cowhand to do. Suddenly reversing direction, Dusty
tilted the gun the opposite way and at the same moment
stepped so that he was to the side of the cowhand.
Before Lee realised what was happening, Dusty changed
direction with his hands once more. The shotgun rose
and Lee trying to retain his hold on the shotgun, heard
its hammers click back and looked into its muzzles.

"Hold it, Jack!" barked Vivian as the other hand
showed signs of taking cards.

"That's real smart," Dusty agreed. "This gun *could*
be loaded. Now you'd best get outside, Mr. Vivian; and
pronto."

Jumping forward, the rancher thrust his man aside
and left the room. Even as he stepped on to the sidewalk, he saw his men looking towards the Silvertip and

swung his eyes in their direction.

On leaving the marshal's office, the Kid glided along the side alley but halted before he reached the street. Cautiously he looked around the corner of the adjacent building and saw the Bradded Box men still sitting their horses in a watchful group, apparently obeying their boss' orders. Turning his eyes the other direction, the Kid saw two men approaching and recognised them as the pair of hardcases Dusty handled in the Silvertip.

"It looks like Gaff went running home for help, Laslo," Bratley was saying in a carrying voice.

"That'd be his way," Laslo replied. "Let's go ask 'em about it afore we go to Red Dora's place."

Suddenly a shape stood on the sidewalk before them. The Kid moved with his usual speed and silence, stepping from the alley and blocking the two Rafter Bar hands' path. He stood with legs apart, balanced lightly, his rifle in both hands and held down across his body.

"Somebody wants to see you back at the Silvertip," he said.

"Who?" growled Bratley.

"Me."

"Get out of our path!" spat Bratley, continuing to move forward.

"Move it," supplemented Laslo, "or we'll tromp you underfoot."

Seeing that the Kid did not intend to step aside, Bratley reached for his gun. Like a flash the Kid stepped forward and made a move almost identical to that tried by Lee in the office; but with the vital difference that neither Bratley nor Laslo possessed Dusty Fog's speed of reaction. Around lashed the rifle to drive its butt with some force into Bratley's Old Stump Blaster-filled belly. Bratley's hand missed the butt of his gun and he rocked backwards, doubling over. Pivoting around the Kid sent the rifle's butt crashing into the side of Laslo's jaw even as the man started to lift his Colt clear. Fortunately for

Laslo, he had not cocked the revolver for the force of
the blow jolted it from his fingers and might have
caused a premature discharge had the hammer been
back. Spinning around, Laslo crashed into the hitching
rail, hung there for a moment and then slid to the
ground.

Despite his border-smuggling youth, the Kid had held
a law badge under Dusty and knew enough of such work
to take no chances when dealing in a deadly situation.
That pair had not been up to ordinary cowhand mis-
chief, but set on causing real bad trouble. With the
Rafter Bar contingent handled, he swivelled around
ready to quieten the Bradded Box crew. He found that
he did not need to bother.

"Hold it, all of you!" Vivian ordered, stepping from
the office.

"Now you're showing sense, Dale," Green commented, following the rancher out. "How are they,
Lon?"

"They've looked better," replied the Kid, looking at
the two Rafter Bar men.

On his knees, Bratley clutched at his belly and
moaned, retching and making a mess on the sidewalk.
Laslo sprawled half on the street and half on the board-
walk, motionless except for the occasional groan.

"Best get them off the street, Garve," Dusty suggested, coming out of the office on the heels of the two
cowhands and deputy sheriff. "And I don't reckon
we'll be needing your hands, Mr. Vivian. Send them
down to the hotel and see they stay there."

"Who's giving the orders around here now, Garve?"
Vivian asked.

"Can't see anything wrong with what Cap'n Fog
says," the marshal replied.

"C——Cap'n Fog?" Vivian gasped, staring at the
small Texan.

"You mean that I jumped Dusty Fog?" gulped Lee. "I need a drink—bad."

"Get it at the hotel," Dusty drawled. "And make sure that it's only one or two. That goes for all of you."

"Yes sir, Cap'n Fog," Lee answered.

Dusty's name had a special meaning amongst cowhands as a defender of their rights against the brutal, corrupt, vicious lawmen who infested most of the Kansas trailend towns. However they also knew that he would brook no interference or opposition to rightful orders when keeping the peace.

"You heard Cap'n Fog," said Vivian. "Do it."

Turning their horses, the cowhands rode off towards the hotel. Green let out a sigh of relief which Vasquez echoed, both men realising that the trouble had been staved off for a time.

"What now?" asked the marshal.

"Get those two off the street first," Dusty answered. "Then we'll go see Mr. Brinded."

"I'll tend to it," Vasquez promised.

"What've you done so far, Dale?" Dusty asked, dropping the chilling "Mr." at the rancher's show of cooperation.

"We searched as best we could in the dark," Vivian replied. "Made plenty of noise, hoping Gaff'd hear and let us know. He didn't."

"It won't be easy, finding him in the night if he's unconscious," Dusty remarked.

"Why'd he come into town tonight?" the rancher asked.

Quickly Dusty told what brought the old timer to town and Vivian shook his head in puzzled manner.

"What do you think?" asked Dusty.

"With anybody but Gaff, I'd say it was just an excuse to come into town. If he went into the Silvertip, there might have been trouble."

"You may as well know now, he had a run-in with the Rafter Bar—Well, not the Rafter Bar, with those two yahoos Lon quietened down."

"Then they could've——."

"Let's wait and see what Mr. Brinded says afore we jump to conclusions," Dusty suggested. "I watched Gaff ride out and Lon kept his eyes on the street for a piece after. Nobody left."

"They could have gone out another way," Vivian pointed out.

"Not unless they've horses somewhere else. Nobody took one from in front of the saloon. How long've you been fussing with the Rafter Bar?"

"I've not been fussing——All right since Fritz Deiter disappeared things have been getting worse. Tonight when Gaff didn't show, I found the beer bottle and knew he'd been to town. It's Rafter Bar's pay night and I wondered if some of them might've jumped him. That Bratley and Laslo're mean."

"They're all put away, Dusty," Green said, emerging from the office. "We'd best see Tom Brinded now."

"Reckon you can trust your boys, Dale?" asked Dusty.

"Sure, but I'll go along to the hotel and make sure they stay there," the rancher answered. "That's unless you figure on something different, Cap'n."

"We'll see Mr. Brinded first," Dusty replied.

Suspicious glances turned towards Green, Dusty and the Kid as they entered the Silvertip. However Brinded's crew had been celebrating and reached the affable stage. Without Bratley and Laslo to prod them on, the remainder of the crew tended to be friendly and less inclined to hunt trouble. Even Brinded managed a grin as Green approached.

"Have a drink, Garve, and you gents," he offered.

"Be right pleased to," Dusty answered.

Like the Bradded Box hands, Brinded's crew admired

Dusty and were not averse to entertaining a man so famous. For his part, Dusty knew how to handle cowhands and soon smoothed away any lingering annoyance the ranch crew might have felt about treatment of Bratley and Laslo. The Kid had a fund of unprintable stories ideally suited to the cowhands' taste and quickly had the group roaring with laughter, then searching for jokes of their own to top his efforts.

Leaving the Kid to keep the cowhands occupied, Dusty and the marshal took Brinded to one side. The rancher showed momentary anger when hearing that two of his men had once more been felled by the Texans and now reposed in the jail. However he saw, without needing to be told, what his men might have started had they not been stopped, so raised no objections.

"What brought Vivian to town?" he growled.

"Gaff didn't get back to the Bradded Box," Dusty replied.

"The hell you say!" Brinded breathed, then a scowl came to his face. "Did he reckon I know something about it?"

"Who'd you've blamed had it been one of your boys and with the Bradded Box in town?" asked Dusty.

"I see what you mean," the rancher admitted. "But none of my boys have left here. Hey though, Bratley and Laslo went out——"

"Before this time?"

"Nope, except to go to the john and they weren't out for more than a few minutes then."

"Anything could've happened on the range," Green commented. "What're we going to do about it, Dusty?"

"I reckon we ought to make a start at searching," Dusty answered. "If we can borrow enough lanterns around town, we can spread the Bradded Box hands and some of the local men out in a line and comb between here and the ranch."

"That's rough country for townsmen to cover in the dark," Brinded put in.

"Sure, but we have to make a start," Dusty answered.

"I've eight boys here, not counting Bratley and Laslo."

"Reckon they'd help?"

"I reckon they would," the rancher said. "Old Gaff was well liked."

CHAPTER FIVE

No Bear Did that Killing

Dusty Fog did his work well and justified Marshal Green's decision to leave him in command. After having demonstrated his ability to handle trouble with bare hands, and shown the devilish speed with which he could draw his matched Colts, he won over the local cowhands with that personal magnetism which made him the born leader and caused other men to follow him. Differences of opinion were forgotten as the Rafter Bar crew, less the two in the cells, offered their assistance. Gaff had been popular before the trouble, which helped gain the necessary assistance; and there was a certain prestige to be gained by saying one had ridden in a posse with the Rio Hondo gun wizard.

While the two lawmen went around town to collect lanterns, Dusty told the posse what he wanted doing. Black coffee sobered up the Rafter Bar hands and shortly before midnight the posse formed up on the edge of town. With the men spread out in a long line, Dusty led them off along the line Gaff ought to have taken while heading for the Bradded Box ranch house.

Riding slowly, directing their lights into any area where the old man might have fallen, the posse crossed the range. They scared up cattle, but the noise of their advance drove off any wild animals that might have been in the vicinity. At last the ranch came into view and there had been no sign of Gaff.

"What do you reckon, Cap'n Fog?" asked Brinded.

"He may have been thrown and's unconscious," Dusty guessed. "If not, he ought to have heard us and let out a yell. We'll make another sweep back to town."

"Not until we've a hot drink inside us," Vivian put in. "And if anybody wants a change of horses, they can pick from the remuda."

Dawn was breaking as the posse returned to Robertstown, but they had still seen no sight of the old timer.

"I can't keep your boys any longer, Tom," Vivian announced.

"The hell you can't," Brinded answered. "We'll keep searching until we find him—or something to tell us where he's gone."

A thought nagged at Dusty, demanding that he accepted the obvious answer to the affair. His eyes went around the posse, seeing tiredness on every face, but no hostility. Gaff's disappearance had smoothed over the two ranches' animosity, given them a common bond at which they might work. But could Dusty rely on the continued good feeling without his presence?

Some men might have called on either the Kid or Marshal Green to give an opinion; with the intention of having others to help share the blame if things went wrong. That had never been Dusty Fog's way.

"Garve," he said "You take the posse again. They can make a more thorough search now it's coming light."

"Aren't you coming along then?" asked the marshal, sounding just a shade concerned; for he knew how much the small Texan's presence had to do with the friendly atmosphere between the two ranch crews.

"Nope, Lon and I are going to look for that cow Gaff saw killed."

"You don't think that he——?" began the marshal.

"It's one answer," Dusty replied. "The noise we made, Gaff ought to have heard us going by. If he didn't, it means he couldn't or was so far off that he missed us. Say, can I borrow that Sharps from off your wall rack?"

"Sure," agreed Green. "Do you reckon there's anything in what Gaff told us about that big cougar?"

"Something moved him for sure," Dusty answered. "And if he did see a cougar that big, I don't fancy tangling with it toting a saddle carbine."

"You could be right there," Green replied. "Say, why not take one of the local hands with you?"

"Sure, it'll save time," Dusty accepted. "Pick one out while I fetch the rifle and some shells."

Following a system thought out by Dusty's father and practised in a number of marshals' offices throughout the range country, Green kept a heavy calibre, single shot rifle as part of his armory. The Winchesters and shotguns on the wall rack provided a handy assault armament should it be needed, but lacked range and power. On occasions, a peace office required a weapon which would hold true over a long distance* and either the Remington or Sharps rifles—designed primarily for buffalo hunting—provided the ideal answer.

Opening a drawer of the desk, Dusty took out a box containing .45/120/550 Sharps bullets. He opened the box and extracted half-a-dozen of the long brass cartridges, noticing that they had solid lead heads which increased their hitting power. After dropping five of the bullets into his pants pocket, Dusty collected the Sharps and fed the sixth into its breech. With the rifle on the

*One such occasion is recorded in THE TROUBLE BUSTERS by J. T. Edson.

crook of his arm, he walked outside. Already the posse had formed up and prepared to move out on an even more thorough search of the area between the ranch and the town. Lee stood with the Kid to one side and turned his eyes in the direction of the small Texan.

"I'm sending Lee along with you, Cap'n," Vivian said. "He knows the range."

"*Gracias*," Dusty replied.

If he felt any doubts as to the wisdom of the rancher's choice, a glance at Lee's eager, smiling face changed it. The young cowhand showed such eagerness to help that it seemed hardly likely he harbored any resentment at the way Dusty had handled him the previous night. If it came to a point, Lee knew he might count himself fortunate to have come off as lightly as he did. Many a man with Dusty Fog's standing and ability would not have hesitated to take harsher measures than those practised by the small Texan.

"Do you know where to take us, Lee?" Dusty asked.

"Near enough, Cap'n," the youngster replied. "Gaff was riding the Wapiti River country yesterday morning, but there're plenty of cutbanks up that way."

"Let's ride then," ordered Dusty. "We can start searching when we get there."

With that he walked to where his seventeen hand paint stallion stood waiting and swung easily into the double girthed Texas saddle even with the Sharps in one hand. The Kid collected his magnificent, huge white stallion, a horse that looked as wild and dangerous as its master. In the white's saddle boot rode the magnificent "One of a Thousand" Winchester Model 1873 rifle the Kid won at the Cochise County Fair when shooting against some of the finest marksmen in the West.* Throwing a glance at the Sharps Dusty held, the Kid felt puzzled. It seemed his *amigo* took Gaff's story seriously

---

*Told in GUN WIZARD by J. T. Edson.

and he did not object to Dusty showing caution.

Trying to act nonchalant and hide his pride at having been selected to act as guide to two such famous men, Lee led the way by the posse and out of town. Instead of following the trail to the Bradded Box, the trio cut off across the range. Lee kept glancing at the Sharps Dusty carried, but did not wish to appear inquisitive by asking questions.

Just as the youngster felt that he could restrain his curiosity no longer, the Kid halted and pointed ahead. Two small dots moved in the high heavens, dots which Lee guessed to be turkey vultures—although he thought, in the range manner, of them as buzzards—and knew what the sight meant. Even as he watched, Lee saw two more specks join the circling pair.

"They're down by the Wapiti River," he said in a hushed, but excited tone.

"Best take us a look then," Dusty replied and touched the paint with his heels to start it moving.

All three men knew that turkey vultures gathered only when food was available and that where the black scavengers circled something lay dead, or dying. In some uncanny manner the vultures knew when the thing on the ground being circled by one of their number was large enough to be worthwhile gathering over. From the way more birds made for the spot, a fair-sized feast lay waiting on the ground.

"Whatever it is," drawled the Kid, studying the birds, "it's dead for sure."

"Can you see it?" asked Lee.

"Nope. But the buzzards are dropping down already. If whatever they're after was even a lil bit alive they'd stay in the air."

As a trainee of the Comanche Dog Soldier lodge, the Kid learned many such things and his knowledge of natural history far surpassed that of a number of acknowledged scientific experts; for he gained it by word of mouth from teachers with generations of practical experience to guide them.

Conversation lapsed and the men concentrated on holding their horses to a mile-eating trot which ate the distance to where the birds dropped groundwards. Coming to the top of a rim, they could see the Wapiti River about a quarter of a mile away. Fed by waters gathered on the hard rocky ground of the Wapiti Hills, the river ran fast, deep and gloomy as the brooding area from which it sprang. Not far from where the men halted, a wide valley cut down to join the river. Valley might be an exaggeration, for its sides rose sheer but at no point more than twenty foot high and in most places considerably less. The vultures appeared to be dropping to something on the far side of the valley and the Kid started his horse moving in their direction. Before he had gone far, he stopped the white stallion and dropped from its saddle to bend down and look at the ground.

"Feller rode up to here late on yesterday afternoon," he announced as he stood up. "Stopped his hoss for a spell, then turned it and headed back the way he came again."

"Gaff was the only one of our crew on this section yesterday," Lee said excitedly. "Maybe this's where he saw that cougar jump the cow."

"We'd best go down there and take a look, Lon," Dusty suggested. "Keep back with me, Lee, so's you don't trample on any sign."

After drawing his rifle from its boot, the Kid advanced on foot. The valley bottom served as a run-off carrying water down to the river in wet periods, but at other times was dry and its bottom covered with short, springy, but highly succulent grass which cattle enjoyed.

Eagerly Lee scanned the ground as he advanced with Dusty. It would be something to tell the boys if he happened to see something before the Kid noticed it; but Lee's dream did not become a reality. While the young man saw exactly the same as the Kid, he could make nothing of what he saw.

"Were some cattle down here," the Kid told the other two. "Grazing peaceable enough, but something spooked them and they lit out at a run."

Lee noticed that a patch of grass seemed to be a slightly different in hue to the normal growth and guessed it meant something; but could not decide what. Dropping to one knee, the Kid bent forward and moved the blades of grass apart in the discolored area then rose and turned to the other two.

"What's up, Lon?" asked Lee.

"Something knocked down a cow here," the Kid replied and rose, staring at the sheer wall of the valley some twenty foot away. "Dragged it over that ways."

"But it couldn't've eaten a whole cow, bones, guts, hide and everything," objected Lee, searching for some sign of the killed animal.

The difference in color became obvious as he looked down. In being brought to the ground, the cow's weight crushed the grass. The short, springy blades began to straighten, but had not yet returned to normal and showed a different shade to the uncrushed growth around them. Looking closer, the young cowhand saw where a line of blood mingled with crushed grass and headed for the wall. After being felled, the cow must have been dragged away—but to where?

Giving a low whistle which brought his horse to him, the Kid vaulted astride and rode towards the twelve foot high wall of the valley. After examining its rim, he turned towards the other two. For once in his life, the Kid allowed surprise to show on his face; although only Dusty read it on the babyishly innocent features.

"Gaff told the truth," said the Kid in a hushed voice.

Looking at the wall, Dusty felt as if an icy hand touched him and could imagine Gaff's feelings at seeing the cougar go up that twelve foot height taking a full

grown cow along. On the face of it, Dusty could not see
how the cougar performed such a feat—unless it did as
Gaff said. The cutbank's wall rose too sheer for the
cougar to back up, hauling the cow after it. Yet on the
lip of the wall showed blood and other signs that the
carcass had been taken over.

"We'd best take a look on top," Dusty said quietly.

"It'd be best," agreed the Kid, looking up at the rim
with a strange expression flickering across his face. "I
sure hope *Ka-Dih's* watching me right now."

Despite the touch of levity as he mentioned the
Comanche's Great Spirit, the Kid felt decidedly uneasy
as he followed Dusty along the wall in search of a place
up which they could take the horses. Everything the
dark young man knew about cougars told him that what
he had seen was all but impossible—yet it had happened.

The bank sloped down at a more gentle angle a short
distance from where the sign showed that the cow had
been hauled over. Turning their horses, the trio rode upwards and halted on the top to study the situation.
Ahead of them, bushes dotted the ground and that,
combined with the rolling nature of the land, prevented
them from seeing the body of the cow. However the
vultures dropping towards the ground gave them an indication of where to go.

"We'll move in on foot," Dusty decided and swung
from his paint's saddle.

While drawing his own rifle from its boot, Lee could
not help glancing in admiration at the magnificent Winchester the Kid produced. Although he had heard of the
fabulous "One of a Thousand" rifle, specially selected
for the trueness of the barrel, given the finest workman-
ship available and made worthy of the title, the Kid's
was the first he had seen. Nor, Lee realised, was the gun
merely a well-made decoration. In the Kid's skilled
hands, it made a very deadly weapon.

While Lee understood the reason for taking their rifles, the cougar must be killed if possible, he failed to see why Dusty brought along the Sharps rifle. A cougar could not be termed a dangerous animal, nor was it particularly hard to kill; so a rifle firing bullets powered by one hundred and twenty grains of powder seemed just a shade heavy when hunting one.

Like most of his kind, Lee failed to look too deeply into the matter on hand. He accepted Gaff's story without going into the details of it too carefully. On the other hand, Dusty gave the matter plenty of thought. If the old timer had seen a cougar act in the manner he described, the animal must be one of exceptional size. True a mountain lion only rarely proved dangerous to man; but that might not apply to one so large that it could kill a full grown cow and——. There Dusty stopped thinking, unable to believe that the cougar could carry its prey up the twelve foot high cut-bank wall. However such a large cat might take some killing, more than possible with the comparatively weak load of the Winchester rifle and carbine he and the Kid carried. So Dusty took the obvious precaution of bringing along a rifle suitable for any emergency.

Dusty's wisdom showed and proved itself soon enough.

Suddenly the bushes ahead of them agitated violently and the vultures which had dropped to the ground took off with startled squawks. Up lunged an animal, but it was not a cougar. No cougar ever stood on its hind legs, or had a body covered with long brown hair tipped with silvery white. The grizzled coloration of the animal's coat, taken with the massive, hump-shouldered body could belong to only one kind of creature—a Texas flat-headed grizzly bear.

"Whooee!" croaked Lee, his rifle suddenly feeling small and inadequate.

At the sound, the bear swung around. It had been disturbed by the arrival of the birds and rose to scare them away from the dead cow that lay beyond the bushes. Seeing a more accessible menace than the fluttering birds, the bear let out a coughing roar and charged, passing through the stout bushes as if they did not exist.

Throwing up his rifle, Dusty took sight. The Sharps felt heavy and awkward compared with his little saddle carbine—or had until that moment. Dusty was not even aware of the added weight or length of the big rifle as he squeezed its trigger, not did he feel the solid kick as the powerful powder charge exploded. At the same instant, the Kid's Winchester spoke, its crack drowned by the deeper roar of the Sharps. So quickly had everything happened that Lee stood frozen, staring at the terrible danger his incautious noise brought about. Even as he thought of moving, two holes appeared as if by magic between the bear's eyes and it started to collapse. Despite the fact that the two bullets tore through the bear's brain and killed it instantly, the impetus of its charge carried the body on to crash down almost at the men's feet.

"A grizzly bear, not a cougar!" Lee gasped. "That was close, Cap'n Dusty. If you hadn't been toting that buffalo gun——."

"Grizzly ain't all that hard to kill," sniffed the Kid, feeling that Lee slighted his part in halting the charge. "Dusty dropped one with his carbine once."

"And don't ever want to do it again," Dusty replied.

"Let's take a look at that cow," the Kid drawled, before Lee could ask questions. The dark Texan knew that Dusty did not like to be reminded of any part of the happenings in the town where his young brother, Danny, died and the small Texan avenged the killing.*

Without waiting for any further comments, the Kid walked by the bear's body and through the bushes. Lee

---

*Told in A TOWN CALLED YELLOWDOG by J. T. Edson.

suddenly realised that further questions on the matter might be unwelcome and cut off the words which rose without saying them. Turning around, he looked to where the horses stood range-tied—with reins trailing free so as to catch under their feet if they tried to move quickly. Fortunately the animals had been far enough back so that the bear's appearance and roar did not scare them into flight. Seeing that their mounts remained ready for use, the youngster followed the Texans through the bushes.

Reaching a small clearing among the bushes, Lee saw what appeared to be a mound of branches and leaves but from which emerged a cow's leg. He had heard of a grizzly burying its prey under such a mound, but had never seen it before. However, before Lee could mention the fact, he saw the Kid halt and look down.

While approaching the mound, the Kid felt something soft and soggy underfoot and saw signs of the earth having been scraped up. Raking at a small heap with toe of his boot, he uncovered a pile of semi-digested grass and an animal's emptied paunch. They had not been tossed there by accident, but clearly dragged from the body and covered over.

"Let's take a look at that critter," he said, his voice sounding puzzled.

Dragging away the leaves and branches exposed the partly eaten body of a large cow. The sight did not surprise Lee, who knew a grizzly mostly dragged its kill to such a place, ate its fill and covered the body over before lying up close by guarding the source of continued food. However the more the Kid saw, the greater became his bewilderment.

From the signs, the Kid concluded that the cow's neck had been broken and he bent to examine the claw marks on the body. Something more caught the Kid's eyes and increased his growing bewilderment. The cow's body had been disembowelled, its internal organs, some of the rib cage and the inner sides of the thighs eaten as well as a considerable portion from the upper shoulder. From studying that the Kid looked at, then measured, the span of the deep fang holes on the cow's neck. He became aware of the sound of voice behind him and realised that Dusty and Lee were talking.

"Looks like we've stopped one drain on our herds, Cap'n," Lee said as the Kid turned toward them.

"How's that?" asked Dusty.

"Killing that bear. I've never known a grizzly stop at one cow after he gets a taste for beef."

"What that got to do with the cow here?" the Kid put in.

"From what I saw happen, that's one bear who won't kill any more cattle."

Jerking his head towards the cow's body, the Kid spoke flatly. "No bear did that killing."

"How do you mean, Lon?" Dusty inquired.

"Like I said. The grizzly didn't kill the cow."

CHAPTER SIX

They Do Say Bullets Are No Use

For a moment Dusty stood looking at the cow's body and thinking of other grizzly bear kills he had seen. From where he stood, he could not see the cow's belly and so missed an important factor.

"The neck's broken," he said. "That's how a grizzly kills."

"Sure," agreed the Kid.

"And the grizzly always hauls its kill to some place like this, covers the body and dens up to guard it."

"Yep."

"Then why do you reckon the bear didn't kill the cow?"

"A bear kills by hitting with its paw," explained the Kid. "It doesn't jump maybe twenty foot from a wall, land on the cow's back, grab hold of its nose with its claws and twist until the neck pops; which's how the cow was killed."

Walking forward, Dusty made a closer examination of the body, paying particular attention to the marks caused by whatever killed the cow sinking claws into flesh to secure a hold. Then his eyes went to the deep fang marks and he swung back to face the Kid.

"I reckon you're right, Lon," he said. "That's a

cougar's way of killing. But I never saw one with jaws that size, or strong enough to bust a full grown cow's neck.''

"That bear was big enough to have done it," Lee objected.

"Sure," the Kid said. "But a bear can't jump more than a few feet."

"The cow was covered over——," Lee began.

"I've seen a cougar kill covered the same way," Dusty interrupted. "Or the grizzly might have done it when he found the body."

"The bear didn't rip open the belly, haul the paunch out and away, then empty it out and bury it," the Kid pointed out. "Fact being, I've never seen a cougar do it either."

Knowing the thoroughness of the Kid's Comanche teachers, Dusty did not question his *amigo's* statement. In fact Dusty had some knowledge in that line himself and knew that little about the affair seemed right. While a grizzly possessed the strength necessary to drag a full grown cow a considerable distance, it could not have climbed that particular part of the wall and dragged its prey up after it; or, if it managed to do so, would have left considerable signs to show it. Some almost forgotten fact began to stir in the Kid's head, trying to break through but not making it. He tried to remember, failed and gave himself over to the pressing business on hand.

"What the hell kind of critter are we dealing with, Lon?" he asked.

"I'm damned if I know," the Kid replied, looking around him as if in search of an answer. "It's not like anything I've ever come acr—— Hell's fire! Look over there, Dusty!"

Following the direction of the Kid's pointing finger, Dusty and Lee studied a sloping, bush and rock dotted rim about a quarter of a mile away. From his expression and tone, they did not know what to expect, but saw

nothing out of the ordinary. Thinking that the Kid
might have spotted some sight of the mysterious animal,
Dusty gave an even more searching examination.

"What is it?" he finally asked.

"I'm not sure and hope I'm wrong," the Kid replied.
"Let's go over and take a closer look."

After collecting their horses, the trio started to ride in
the direction of whatever had caught the Kid's eye. Not
until they had covered a hundred or more yards of the
distance between the dead cow and the slope did either
Dusty or Lee see the black speck beyond a rock and they
had to ride closer before being able to recognise it. Once
they did so, both men understood the reason for the
Kid's agitation. It said much for the Kid's superb eye-
sight that he not only spotted the thing but recognised it
as a high-heeled riding boot from such a distance.

Hoping against hope, the three men galloped closer.
Remembering what had happened the last time they approached a body, Dusty insisted that they halted the
horses and advanced on foot. With their rifles held
ready, the trio walked cautiously towards the rock. Gaff
lay sprawled on the ground face down, his Winchester a
short distance away.

Dusty rested his rifle on the rock and dropped to one
knee beside the still shape and Lee joined him. The Kid
moved straight past the other two, his eyes scouring the
surrounding area and his Winchester gripped firmly.
After ensuring that there was no immediate danger, he
lowered his gaze to the ground and began to read the
signs left the previous night.

One glance told Dusty that he could do nothing for
the old cowhand. Gaff lay too stiffly to be alive, rigor
mortis had already set in. From the unnatural way the
head tilted Dusty guessed the neck was broken. However he could see no sign of teeth or claw marks upon
the old timer and guessed the fatal injury came from
Gaff's landing on the ground.

"What do you make of it, Lon?" Dusty asked.

"His hoss reared and threw him," the Kid replied.

"But he was riding the steadiest hoss in our remuda," Lee objected.

"The sign's plain enough here, boy," said the Kid gently. "He came up here riding peacable enough. Then the hoss reared, pitching him off and took to running like the devil after a yearling."

"Which means something scared it," Dusty concluded.

"Scared it bad," agreed the Kid. "Something that come out of the bushes there with a rush."

Scooping up the Sharps, Dusty rose and looked around. "Did it come back again, Lon?"

"Not that I can see. It took off after the hoss and kept going."

"Reckon you can trail it?"

"I can sure as hell make a try," promised the Kid quietly.

"What was it, Kid?" asked Lee, staring down at the body of the man who taught him everything he knew about the cowhand's trade.

"There's no way of knowing for sure," admitted the Kid. "No clear sign, but all I can see points to it being the biggest cougar I've ever come across."

Silence dropped on the trio as they stood and looked around them then down at the body. All could imagine the scene; Gaff riding along nursing his rifle, then the sudden appearance of the enormous cougar, followed by the panic-filled rearing of the horse which flung the old man out of his saddle and sent him crashing to the ground.

"How did old Gaff bust his neck?" groaned Lee.

"He must have landed badly," Dusty replied.

"Not Gaff!" Lee insisted.

"He wasn't getting any younger," the Kid pointed out.

"Old as he was, Gaff could still take the bed-springs out of a snuffy one," Lee replied. "He's been thrown before and never done more than bruise himself."

"There's a difference in riding a snuffy one in a corral and being tossed by surprise, Lee," Dusty said. "Most times a man can feel himself going and be ready for it when he's on a bucking horse."

Yet even as he tried to give the youngster comfort, Dusty saw objections to his words. He had thought that Gaff, riding a steady horse, might be dozing in the saddle; a cowhand often did, relying on his horse to take him home. On second thought Dusty discarded the idea. Gaff had not been headed for his home ranch, but came up this way in search of proof that his eyes did not play tricks on him. The fact that he carried his rifle instead of having it in the boot proved he did more than merely ride home. An old timer, raised in the days of Indian raids, would never relax and doze in his saddle at such a time.

Unexpected as it must have been, the sight of the cougar would scare the horse into rearing, but a man of Gaff's training ought to have stuck in the saddle or broken his fall when thrown. Unless something more happened to paralyze his mind in the vital instant when it should have been ordering his limbs to act and soften the landing. The sight of a cougar, even one of exceptional size, should not scare a hard old cuss like Gaff; especially when he had already seen it once and rode with the intention of finding it.

"Let's go, Lon," Dusty said.

"We'll find that damned cougar if it takes a month," Lee growled.

"Not you, Lee," Dusty replied. "I want you to go into town and tell the marshal what's happened. You know this range better than either Lon or me and can make better time."

Even wild with anger and grief over Gaff's death, Lee

could see the wisdom in Dusty's words. Slowly the objections died unsaid and he looked down once more at the stiff, still form of his old friend.

"How about—him?" the youngster asked. "We can't just leave him lying there, those buzzards——."

"I'll tend to it," promised the Kid. "Loan me your bandana."

While removing his bandana, Lee watched the Kid bend and untie Gaff's from around the distorted neck. Using the old man's bandana to cover the head, the Kid placed a rock on each corner. Then he took the cloth offered by Lee and fastened it by two corners on a nearby bush, leaving it to sway and blow in the breeze.

"Buzzards are mighty suspicious critters," he told the other two. "They'll not come down while that's moving."

"Make a fast run to town," Dusty ordered. "And ask Garve Green to bring any cat-hounds that he can lay his hands on."

"Sure," the youngster replied dubiously. "How about you, Cap'n?"

"We'll take the trail, see if we can find that damned cougar."

Lee nodded his head. Much as he wanted to help follow and take revenge on the animal, whatever it might be, that caused Gaff's death, he realised that his duty lay in arranging for the body's collection and return to the ranch for burial.

"Tell Joe Vasquez I'll blaze the trail for him," the Kid remarked. "We'll not be travelling fast and they'll catch up with us."

"Are there any cat-hounds around town?" Dusty asked.

"Major Calverly has four blueticks over to his spread," Lee replied. "Only I don't know if he'll bring 'em out to help us."

"Maybe Garve Green'll be able to persuade him," Dusty said. "Happen the Major's like every other hound-dog man I've met, he'll jump at the chance of helping run down a cougar as big as this one."

In no way was Dusty slighting his *amigo's* tracking ability by sending word for a pack of hounds to help hunt down Gaff's killer. The Kid had few peers in following a trail, but could only move slowly on so difficult a task. Using hounds would speed the search and give them a better chance of coming up to the animal— Dusty held back from thinking of it as a cougar—they sought.

Never had the Kid's skill been given such a test. Among the fighting Indian tribes, the most severe test of a young brave's ability had always been to track down and kill a cougar and only a few succeeded in doing so. After a final glance around, the Kid turned to Dusty.

"Let's go," he said.

Already Lee had mounted and the youngster started his horse moving in the direction of Robertstown. Much as he hated walking, Dusty knew he must do so. The Kid could never follow so difficult a trail from the back of his horse or at any more than a slow walk.

Moving slowly, his eyes studied the ground some distance ahead and noted any slight variations. A stone overturned, a piece of scuffed earth, crushed down grass, all those helped the Kid. Using his knowledge, the Kid reconstructed what happened the previous night. After missing with its rush, the cougar still kept after the horse for a time. Realising at last that it could not catch up to the horse, the cougar halted, stood for a time watching its departing prey, then swung off and went off at an angle to where Gaff's body lay.

While able to follow the tracks, the Kid never saw a clear indication of the kind of animal he trailed. He hoped to find a clear track, enabling him to see the shape of the animal's foot, but this did not materialize. However by gauging the distance between the feet he formed an impression of the size and could even make a guess at the weight. The estimation surprised him, but he felt sure he was right in it. From the stride, he figured the cougar to be around six foot six long, not counting the tail. The weight puzzled him. A cougar tended to be a long, slender animal, but unless he missed his guess the one he trailed would weigh around three hundred pounds.

"I've never seen a big Texas cat that went over two hundred," Dusty commented when the Kid mentioned his findings. "And even those real big puma in the Rocky Mountains don't reach two fifty according to Kerry Barran."

"Reckon he knows as much about them as anybody," drawled the Kid, for the man in question acted as a professional hunting guide in addition to running a successful horse ranch and made the Rocky Mountains his favorite area.* "Only this cat weighs just like I say."

Dusty had sufficient faith in his companion to accept the estimate and worked out what the figures meant. With a head and body length of six foot six, the trail ought to take the cat to at least nine foot. Even so, the normal cougar would not be so heavy at that size.

"I suppose it is a cougar we're after, Lon," Dusty said.

"What else could it be?" the Kid replied. "A bear's claws'd show all the time, not just when they dig in before a charge."

"How about one of those spotted cats down in Mexico, jaguars?"

"*El tigre*," drawled the Kid, using the Mexican name.

*Kerry Barran's story is told in THE BIG HUNT by J. T. Edson.

"I don't know, they do grow to a fair size."

"Only Gaff would have noticed the spots," Dusty said.

"There's that," agreed the Kid.

Letting the matter drop, they moved on in silence and with the horses following like well-trained hound-dogs. Dusty kept behind and to one side of the Kid, watching the range ahead and allowing his *amigo* to concentrate on the tracks without fear of an ambush. The direction they took led them in a half circle and down towards the distant river. Beyond the river lay the brooding, rocky slopes of the Wapiti Hills. There was something sinister about the barren hill range, a feeling that evil reigned among them. Dusty tried to shake off the feeling that perhaps they trailed a creature unknown on the Western ranges, but the gloomy hills—not even the well-risen sun made them look any more cheerful or pleasant—helped to keep the feeling going. Apparently it affected the Kid too; possibly more so, as at such a time his Indian blood was well to the fore.

"I'll be starting to believe in spirit-critturs soon," he growled, halting glaring at the Hills. "They do say bullets are no use against them."

"Happen we come up with it," Dusty answered. "I'll for sure see if they told the truth."

Another mile fell behind them and at last the Kid halted. He pointed to the ground, but Dusty could read little or nothing from it.

"Crouched down here," the Kid explained. "Started to make a stalk on something or other." He pointed to some marks. "Here's the claw marks, just like back there. Critter dug them in ready to shove off with a rush."

Not far ahead the earth had been churned up and blood showed but the tracks ended abruptly, showing that the animal had sprung from the ground at its intended victim. Beyond the scuffle lay the unmistakable marks left by a heavy body being dragged along the ground.

Topping a rise, they saw the victim—a large bull wapiti.

"God damn it, Dusty!" the Kid breathed. "I've seen a full grown black bear killed by a bull elk."

Again the eerie feeling crept over Dusty and he nodded. A full grown range cow could not be termed an easy mark, but a bull wapiti was an even more dangerous proposition. As a member of the deer family, the wapiti had speed and agility. It also weighed upwards of nine hundred pounds and carried long powerful antlers with six sharp-pointed tines a side *and* knew how to use them. Even a grizzly bear, undisputed monarch of the Great Plains before the coming of reliable firearms, only took on a bull wapiti as a last resort.

"No sign of the—the cougar," said the Kid, searching the surrounding area. "Most likely laid up after feeding."

"Could be up one of those trees, among the bushes, anywhere," Dusty replied. "Let's go down and see."

Knowing that a cougar would always run from human beings, Dusty and the Kid still took no chances as they advanced towards the kill. That animal they followed showed a lot of un-cougar habits; enough to make the Texans wary. They reached the body without incident and halted to examine it.

"Right foreleg's bust," the Kid said. "Bent inwards and most likely happened when that critter jumped it."

"Could be," Dusty replied, wondering why the wapiti did not react fast enough to defend itself against the charge. "It's been gutted like the other. Eaten the same way, too. Thighs, heart, liver, ribs. But it's not been covered over."

"Likely the bear did that, drove off the cougar afore it ate its fill. That was why it tried to jump Gaff and kept moving. It was hungry and hunting.''

The thought that the bear could chase their mysterious prey off its kill gave the Texans some slight relief. If a bear could scare it, then a Sharps rifle bullet ought to be real potent medicine. Dusty looked at the Kid and grinned.

"It's those damned hills,'' the small Texan said.

"They're sure scarey,'' agreed the Kid. "No wonder that the Apaches wouldn't go near them. The tracks go off towards them rocks.''

For all their relief, the Texans did not relax as they approached the rocks. Maybe that cougar had been chased off by a bear, but it could be dangerous if cornered and possessed the deadly armament of its kind in addition to sufficient size and weight to make its presence felt.

The tracks led under the shelter of an overhanging rock and from the signs the big cat had rested there, but was gone before the Texans arrived. Not long gone, or the Kid missed his guess. Bending, he raked together some hairs and turned to show them to Dusty.

"Look like a cougar's all right,'' the small Texan drawled. "Only I've never seen one do much moving around in daylight. Did we scare him off?''

"Nope, he pulled out maybe a quarter of an hour back, headed for the river. Happen the wind holds from him to us, we might catch up.''

"Let's make a try,'' Dusty said.

Taking the trail once more, the Texans followed it at a slightly faster pace. Before they could cover a hundred yards up a slope which probably overlooked the river— they could hear the sound of the water—something happened to halt them in their tracks.

A roar shattered the air, yet of a kind the like of which the Kid had never heard before. It was not the deep, awesome bellow of a grizzly bear, nor the saw-rasping note of *el tigre* in a rage, but still a sound charged with menace—and not any noise he had ever heard made by a cougar.

"What the hell——?" he began.

Dusty did not reply. Memory rushed back to the small Texan as he recollected where last he heard such a sound. Impossible as it seemed, he recognised the roar and knew what made it. He also could guess how Gaff came to die and why the bull wapiti failed to react in time to defend itself.

There was no time to explain theories to the Kid, Dusty realised as he heard another sound mingled with the roar from beyond the rim. Springing forward, forgetting his aching feet, he went bounding up the slope and prayed that he might reach the top in time.

CHAPTER SEVEN

A Tolerable Hunk of Man

"You sure can pick a pleasant trail, Mark," commented Miss Martha Jane Canary, eyeing the surrounding walls, sheer cliffs, barren slopes and iron hard earth of the Wapiti Hills with some disgust.

"It saves three days riding, Calam," Mark replied. "Which same I need some saving, Cousin Beauregard sure throws a whing-ding when he celebrates."

"You late meeting up with Dusty?" asked the girl.

"Nope, but I sure will happen I had to go round."

On the face of it, Mark Counter had little to fear from Dusty Fog either physically or as an employee of the OD Connected ranch.

Sat astride his huge bloodbay stallion, Mark's six foot three inches of height did not show, although he towered well over his companion. Nothing could hide the great spread of his shoulders and his enormous biceps showed under the material of his expensive tan, made-to-measure shirt. He slimmed down at the waist curving out two long, powerful legs, giving him the muscular development of a Hercules. Topping his golden blond hair, a costly white J. B. Stetson shielded an almost classically handsome face, tanned, intelligent and strong. Around his waist hung a gunbelt tooled by a

master craftsman, its holsters designed to give the max-
imum speed to withdrawing the matched ivory handled
Colt Cavalry Peacemakers. A man with such a development need not fear even the deadly techniques used by
Dusty Fog.

Nor would being fired cause Mark any discomfort.
While something of a dandy dresser—his clothing now
set cowhand fashion as during the War it commanded
the respect of the dress-conscious bloods of the Confederate Army—he could claim to be a master at cattle
work; some said even better than Dusty Fog. Such a
man could easily find employment. If it came to a point,
Mark had the means to set himself up in a business without working for other men. The third son of a rich
Texas rancher, he was wealthy in his own right due to a
maiden aunt leaving him her considerable fortune when
she died. For all that, Mark preferred to ride as a hand
not just an ordinary working hand true, but a member
of Ole Devil's floating outfit and right bower to Dusty
Fog.

Folk talked of Mark's strength, his skill in a brawl,
but few enough could say of his ability with his Colts.
Those who *knew*, and they numbered some of the top
names in the gun-fighting line, claimed Mark to be second only to Dusty Fog in speed and accuracy. So it
seemed that Mark need fear nothing from being late.

Since their first meeting, down in Mexico shortly after
the end of the War,* Mark had come to know how
Dusty hated lack of punctuality. The small Texan had
no desire to delay his return to the Rio Hondo and Mark
possessed sufficient loyalty to the brand to agree with
Dusty. On visiting his cousins' ranch, Mark found a
wedding imminent and could hardly ride on without enjoying the celebrations. As he told Miss Canary, his
cousin's hospitality tended to be lavish and Mark found

*Told in THE YSABEL KID by J. T. Edson.

himself with only the bare minimum of time to reach the rendezvous at Robertstown.

Mark's cousin told how one could go through the Wapiti Hills, provided he took water and food along. A trail wide enough for use by a wagon passed through the hills; but was not used due to lack of water and grazing. Knowing that the forty mile trip would take two to three days by wagon, Mark figured he could do it in one on his horse. So he loaded supplies of water and food on a pack pony before leaving his cousin's place and rode out secure in the knowledge that the short-cut would bring him to Robertstown in good time.

Meeting Miss Canary on the trail came as something of a surprise, especially when he learned that she headed in his direction. Of course, having her along tended to be a mixed blessing; but Mark enjoyed her company and not because she could claim to be something of a famous person in her own right.

Not that many folks would recognise the name Martha Jane Canary. Say Calamity Jane, though in any saloon, freight outfit, trail drive camp or army post west of the Mississippi and there would be no doubt who was meant. Calamity Jane, many were the stories of her exploits and varied the tales of how she came to rise to fame.

Shorn of all romanticism, Calamity had been left in a St. Louis convent by her mother, fled it at sixteen and became accepted as a member of Dobe Killem's freight outfit. From the drivers, she learned to use a gun, hitch, care for and handle a six-horse wagon team and use the long lashed bull whip which was the freight hauler's tool, weapon and badge of office. The name Calamity came from her ability to find trouble and a penchant to become involved in hair-yanking brawls while visiting saloons, generally managing to entangle her fellow drivers in the ensuing fuss. Despite that habit, she had their respect; gained by her courage, good hearted generosity and many other sterling qualities.

After several hectic meetings, Mark felt much the same as the Killem outfit about the girl; but he regarded her as a mixed blessing. Of course it seemed highly unlikely that they would meet any trouble along that barren trail and Miss Canary's business ought to keep her too busy in Robertstown to land them in a saloon fuss.

A battered U.S. cavalry kepi perched jauntily on her short mop of curly red hair. Health, zest for living and a lively sense of humor showed on her freckled face, which, while not truly beautiful, was attractive enough to draw glances in any company. If her looks did not, then her choice of clothing would. The weather being warm, she had left off her fringed buckskin jacket and fastened it to the cantle of her fancy buckskin gelding's saddle. Tight enough for her to appear molded into it, the man's tartan shirt emphasized the round fullness of her bosom and was open low enough at its neck to remove any doubts as to her sex. Her levis pants looked like they had been bought a mite too small and shrunk in washing. Cinched about her trim waist, the pants showed the rich curves of her hips and shapely thighs. Indian moccasins decorated her feet. Around her waist hung a gunbelt with an ivory handled Navy Colt, rechambered to take metal cartridges, butt forward in her holster. Thrust into her waist band, she carried the long-lashed bull whip specially built for her and in the use of which she could claim to be something of a maestro.

Sat astride her horse, she was five foot seven of rich femininity and defiance of convention; a girl born with a love of adventure and possessing sufficient courage to go out to look for it.

"If we'd gone around, it'd've been three *nights* on the trail," she pointed out.

"I thought of that too," grinned Mark. "Which's one of the reasons why I'm going through here."

"But this way we'll only have one more night."

"Yeah!" agreed Mark pointedly.

"I'm damned if you're not getting old," sniffed
Calamity. "Time was——."

After following the bottom of a valley for a time, the
trail had climbed up to run along one side. On either
side of the valley was too steep for any horse to traverse
it, with jagged rocks waiting to tear into flesh should
such a foolish attempt be made. The trail was safe
enough, with sufficient width for two riders side by side
to feel no concern. Not far away, the valley curved with
its other side hidden from the approaching riders. Certain sounds from around the curve ceased Calamity's
words.

Neither Mark nor Calamity needed to ask what
caused that dull rumbling noise. Voices shouted, a splin-
tering crash sounded followed by a deeper rumbling and
the very ground under their horses' hooves shook.
Without a word, the girl and Mark set their horses forward at a better pace.

Turning the corner, they found a near disaster had
taken place. Something caused a rock slide from above.
One huge slab leaned against the valley side and effectively blocked the trail; but it caused little actual damage. Closer at hand, more of the fall had struck the rear
of a light, two horse wagon and the combined weight
tore out a considerable section of the trail. Already the
wagon had fallen into the hollow caused by the trail's
collapse and dragged the horses after it. Three men, one
of them on foot, and a woman were between the wagon
and the approaching pair. The riders struggled to regain
control of their horses and the other man rose after having leapt clear once he felt the wagon going. None of the
party made any move to try to save the horses from
being dragged over the edge and down the steep slope to
an agonizing death.

Even as he passed the riders, with hardly a glance at
them, Mark knew he could not prevent the horses being

hauled to their doom. There would be no chance of
jerking out the pin and freeing the doubletree from the
wagon. To do so meant going over the edge, standing on
the wagon then jumping clear. Given a reasonably safe
surface on which to land, Mark might have tried it. To
jump from a moving wagon on to the bare rock of the
slope could only end in disaster.

Reluctantly Mark decided what he must do. Leaving
his bloodbay's saddle, he landed some ten foot away
from the two team horses. Terrified eyes rolled at him as
the animals felt themselves being pulled backwards.
Already their hindlegs had started downwards and their
fore hooves churned desperately to drag themselves and
the dead weight of the wagon back to safety. A vain and
losing fight with death, at its end.

Down dropped Mark's right hand, fingers closing on
the ivory handle of the off side Colt. In that flowing,
smooth motion which showed the difference between
the average performer and the truly great, Mark's Colt
left leather and lined with the minimum of movement.
Flame lashed from the seven and a half inch barrel and a
bullet ripped home in the center of the outer horse's
head. Thumbing back the hammer as the barrel kicked
up, Mark cocked the Colt and shot again. Fast though
the two explosions followed each other, his second bullet struck the remaining horse in the best spot for an
instant kill. Just as the lead struck the second animal,
the wagon gave a jerk and dragged them both over the
shattered edge of the trail. Down it lurched, barely
slowed by the dead weight trailing behind it. One wheel
flew off, timbers shattered. The canvas canopy disinte-
grated as the wagon rolled over. The two horses followed the wagon down. Although the doubletree parted
company, it would not have happened soon enough to
save the horses from frightful injury had they been
alive; nor could they have survived on that steep slope.

So Mark's action saved them from a painful, possibly slow, death.

For all that, the blond giant hated the necessity to kill two fine animals. Turning, he looked at the trio who had accompanied the wagon. His face held no condemnation, for he realised that things probably happened too swiftly for there to be any escape or chance of preventing the wagon going over. Even had the driver remained on the box, he could not halt the downward plunge and could hardly be blamed for saving his own life.

Mark's eyes went to the men first and received something of a surprise. The wagon looked like the type used by a ranch's cook, but the three men were not the usual run of cowhands. In fact, Mark found himself hard put to place them. Medium in height, stocky, swarthy skinned, they looked of Latin birth, but the language as they dropped from their saddles the better to control their horses was not Spanish. Dressed in a hybrid mixture of range and town, their clothes told nothing. All the trio carried knives in their belts, but gave no sign of wearing revolvers.

Being more used to the variety of races hired to construct railroads, Calamity recognised the men as Italians. When their cold, black eyes turned her way, the girl felt pleased that her whip rode handy to her grip and that Mark Counter stood at her side.

After swinging from the saddle of her fine dun mare, the woman of the party tossed her reins to the driver and looked to where Mark holstered his Colt. Although as tall as Calamity, the woman was slimmer. Honey blonde hair framed a good-looking face which showed arrogance and pride. Her hat, a flat-topped Stetson, doeskin jacket and divided skirt, white satin blouse and calf-high riding boots had cost plenty, hinting of wealth beyond that of the usual run of ranch owners. In her gauntleted right hand she held a riding quirt, tapping it against her thigh as she studied the blond giant.

"Sorry I had to do that, ma'am," Mark said. "It was the only way."

"I understand," she replied. "The rock slide took us by surprise. Fortunately I was past when it struck."

Mark could not place the accent. While undoubtedly British, it did not have the sound of such upper-class Englishmen that he knew. Nor did it carry any of the dialects heard among the poorer immigrants he had met. Something between the two, perhaps, he concluded.

One thing was for sure, Calamity did not like the woman. That showed in the red head's sudden intake of breath and snorted out comment as she stood holding her own and Mark's horse.

"Your driver nearly wasn't so fortunate."

"Possibly not," replied the blonde, sounding as if the thought never occurred to her and was of no importance now that it had. Again she turned her attention to Mark. "Thank you, sir. I——The trail is blocked."

"It looks that way, ma'am," Mark agreed, gazing over the damaged section to the huge rock beyond.

While it would be possible to cross the ledge remaining after the sweeping away of most of the trail, the rock leaned at an angle which made it impassable. Mark let out an annoyed grunt. Already half a day had passed and to retrace his path would make him late in arriving at Robertstown. It seemed that the blonde also had some urgency in her journey.

"I must get back and tell my husband what has happened," she said. "The supplies I was to collect are urgently needed."

"Let's take a look over there, Calam," Mark said.

"Sure," Calamity agreed and thrust the reins into the blonde's hand. "Hold these for us, girlie."

Cold fury showed on the other woman's face, but

Calamity ignored her and walked after Mark over the narrow stretch. With an angry gesture, the blonde passed the reins to her driver and followed the other two.

"Couldn't get the hosses through, even without saddles," Calamity remarked, looking at the V-shaped gap under the rock. "Might lever it over, only we've nothing to use as a lever. No chance of getting ropes around it and hauling it over."

"Blow it out of the way," suggested the blonde.

"What with?" Calamity snorted.

"Strip the heads off bullets and use their powder."

"At twenty-eight and forty grains a bullet, that'd need a heap of hulls," Calamity sniffed. "And even if we got enough powder, touching it off might bring the rest of the wall down."

"But I must reach my husband and inform him of the loss," the blonde said, replacing a glare of animosity with a pleading expression as she swung from Calamity to Mark. "Is there nothing you can do, Mister——."

"Counter, ma'am. Mark Counter, at your service."

"I am the Countess Katherine Giovanni. My husband owns the old Spanish mission and it is essential that I return to make other arrangements for collecting supplies as soon as possible."

Knowing little or nothing of the local geography, Mark felt puzzled over the mention of the old Spanish mission. Possibly there had been one built on the edge of the Wapiti Hills; many such were turned into ranch houses, being of solid and lasting construction. He would have thought Robertstown a nearer source of supply than coming through the Wapiti Hills, but realized that the Countess might have personal reasons for not using the town.

Putting aside his thoughts on the woman's words, Mark studied the rock. Its under side looked fairly flat, the upper surface making a large, irregular dome. If the rock could be stood erect, the weight of the domed side ought to tip it over the edge of the trail. Only one problem remained to be solved, standing the rock erect. Unless Mark missed his guess, that slab of rock weighed all of nine hundred pounds and maybe more.

Carefully Mark eased himself under the gap. Crouching slightly, his forehead against the wall and back to the rock, he tentatively tested the weight. If anything, he undercalled it at nine hundred pounds. However a man never knew what he could do until he made a try.

"Can my men help?" called the Countess as Mark relaxed before making his attempt.

"There's no room," Mark replied.

"But surely he can't——," the Countess began, addressing Calamity for the first time.

"He's sure as hell going to try," the red head replied.

Taking up his position, Mark placed his hands against the side of the valley. The crushed position in which he had to work did nothing to make his task easier, but he gritted his teeth and began to exert all his strength, thrusting backwards with his legs and shoulders, shoving against the unyielding valley side with his hands. Across the damaged section of the trail one of the men gave a jeering laugh and made some comment Calamity could not understand. Turning her head, the Countess hissed an order in the same language and the men lapsed into silence.

Ignoring the others, Calamity stood and watched Mark. Sweat already burst out over his face and soaked his shirt, telling of the tremendous strain his efforts placed on his giant physique. It seemed impossible that one man might achieve anything against the huge, inanimate mass. Yet at their first meeting Calamity had watched Mark raise the rear wheel of her wagon from a gopher hole into which it sank*; and on another occa-

*Told in TROUBLED RANGE.

sion saw him hoist a six hundred pound dumb-bell over his head.* All in all, Calamity mused Mark Counter was a tolerable hunk of man but he might be biting off more than he could chew this time.

For seconds nothing appeared to be happening, other than Mark straining to no avail. Then, even as Calamity thought he must give up the attempt, she saw a faint gap where previously the rock rested against the almost sheer side of the valley above the trail. So slowly that the eye could barely register it, the gap widened; one inch, two, three, each won at the cost of the Lord only knew what effort on the blond giant's part. Calamity stood rigid, hands so tightly clenched that they hurt—or would have had her full attention not been concentrated on trying to will Mark to further success.

"I'll call my men," the Countess said in a hushed voice, her eyes never leaving Mark.

"Leave them be," Calamity replied. "And keep quiet!"

Once again fury showed on the blonde's face, but she stood still and fought it down. Her mouth, opened to say something, closed without speaking. After the brief, low-spoken warning, Calamity paid no attention to the Countess. While the men might help, possibly their arrival and taking up position would distract the blond giant. If Mark once lost control, the whole enormous weight would crush down on top of him. The base of the rock had slipped while being raised and was now so far forward that the top would no longer catch on the valley wall should it swing back to its original position.

Slowly the gap at the top widened. Mark braced himself and took the strain, supporting the rock on his shoulders as he removed his hands from the wall. No longer could he gain any advantage by forcing with his hands on the wall and must take the chance of getting

*Told in THE FORTUNE HUNTERS.

his arms back to the rock. It was a time of deadly danger and a low gasp left Calamity as she saw the rock quiver in the direction from which it came. Throwing his strength into the effort, Mark held firm and his arms moved into position. Saw-rasping grunts left him as he tried to draw breath and gathered himself for a final attempt. Drawing on all his reserves of energy, he strained back, legs thrusting against the hard surface of the trail, shoulders and arms shoving at the rock. Slowly it rose to fully erect, quivered as if in final attempt to resist the Texan's will. Once erect, the domed upper surface took control, beginning to tip the remainder over and outwards. Relieved of the strain as the rock tipped over the trail's edge and plummeted downwards, Mark staggered backwards and looked like following into the rock-strewn death-trap valley below.

CHAPTER EIGHT

I Don't Want to Change My Boss

Springing forward, Calamity caught Mark by the wrist. Digging in her heels, she flung her weight back in an effort to stop the Texan's rearward movement. Two arms locked around Calamity's waist from behind as the Countess saw the danger. On the very edge of the trail, with that killing slope behind him, Marks progress halted. The Countess screamed out orders for her men to help, but before any of them could obey Calamity swung Mark to safety.

Exhausted and spent by his tremendous effort, the blond giant sank to hands and knees. He fought to breathe, drawing air into lungs which seemed to be burning and his giant frame shook with the reaction. Releasing Calamity, the Countess hurried across the narrow stretch. On reaching her horse, she opened its saddle pouch and produced a bottle. Retracing her steps, she dropped to one knee by Mark as he sat on the trail. She dragged the cork from the bottle and looked at Calamity who held out a hand.

"Either give him a drink, or let me do it," the red head ordered.

"I have no glass," replied the Countess.

"I don't reckon Mark'll mind," said Calamity and took the bottle to hold it to Mark's mouth.

Drinking deeply, the Texan's exhaustion did not prevent him feeling surprised at what he tasted. Not the raw bite of whiskey, although the bottle's shape would have told him not to expect it had he been his usual self; what Mark drank proved to be wine—and real good wine too. It sank through him, steadying the shivers that ran through his body and soothing the raw pain in his chest.

"How'd you feel, Mark?" asked Calamity.

"Better."

"Then get up and stop faking."

"Lend a tired old man a shoulder then," Mark suggested.

Using both women as a support, Mark rose to his feet. Only for a moment did he feel a whirl of dizziness, then his superb physical condition began to throw off the effects of his tremendous feat of strength. He felt the Countess' hands on his arm, testing the size of his bicep, while she looked him over with more than casual interest.

"That was truly a great feat you performed," she purred, eyes on his face.

"I want to get through there, too, ma'am," Mark answered. "Thanks for the wine. It's as good as I've ever tasted."

"You are acquainted with wine?"

"I've drunk enough of it to know good from bad," Mark replied.

"You'll know something else happen you're late hitting Robertstown," Calamity put in. "And your *husband'll* likely want to know about that wagon, *Mrs.*——."

At the emphasized mention of her husband, the Countess jerked her hand from Mark's arm and fury once more showed when Calamity said "Mrs." For a moment her eyes locked with the red head's and read challenge in Calamity's level gaze. Abruptly the Countess swung around and stalked across the narrow stretch to where her men stood waiting.

"You're a mean, ornery female, Calam," grinned Mark.

"Takes one to know one, which same she surely recognised me," the girl replied. "Watch her, Mark. She's for sure a man-eater."

"There's some might start pouring salt and pepper on themselves ready," drawled the blond giant.

"She's too skinny," Calamity objected.

"They do say the nearer the bone, the sweeter the meat."

"I should've let you fall over the edge. Maybe bouncing down there on your fool head'd've pounded some sense into it."

"You know me, Calam gal. I like 'em with a mite more meat and without a husband."

"Now I'm pleased I didn't let you go over. What the hell's she fixing to do?"

On rejoining her men, the Countess snatched her horse's reins and started to lead it towards the damaged section of the trail. At first the dun followed quietly enough, but on approaching the area where the trail fell away showed signs of hesitation. Even then all might have been well had the Countess used patience and good horse sense. Seeing Calamity watching, the blonde felt hot anger at the dun's refusal and gave a jerk at its head. Instead of compelling obedience, the move caused the dun to draw back and rear. Never the best-tempered or most patient of women, the Countess reached boiling point. Snarling obscenities which, being in English, Mark and Calamity could understand, she swung back her right arm and slashed the quirt savagely at the dun.

"Quit that, you stupid——!" Calamity shouted and darted across the narrow piece before Mark could stop her.

Catching the Countess's right arm as it rose again, Calamity jerked her from the horse then shoved her away to crash into the slope at the side of the trail. One of the three men let out a low hiss, turned and started to jerk the rifle from his saddleboot. Following Calamity up fast, Mark saw the move and opened his mouth to yell a warning. Before he could speak, Calamity saw her danger and took action.

Like a flash her right hand crossed to, gripped the whip's handle and slid it from the waistband. In the same move, she snapped the hand forward and up, sending the lash uncoiling in the man's direction. Used in that manner, Calamity could not gain full power; for which the man might have counted himself very lucky. With an explosive "Whap!" the tip of the whip caught the back of the man's right hand and batted the rifle from it. Although pain knifed through him, he suffered less damage than could easily have happened. If the whip had landed with full force, it would have ripped a gash in his flesh and cut through to the bone.

Giving a low, savage hiss, the Countess sprang forward and swung up the quirt to launch a blow at Calamity. Pivoting, the red head threw up her whip, its handle catching the quirt before the lash could reach her. Calamity expected no difficulty in holding off the blonde and it came as something of a shock to feel the other's strength. Despite her expensive clothes and fancy dude accent, there were hard muscles in the slim frame and a strength almost equal to Calamity's own. Almost, but not quite. With a surging heave, Calamity shoved the Countess away from her again.

"All right, girlie!" Calamity hissed. "If you want to play——"

"Hold it all of you!"

Mark knew Calamity well enough to be aware that he must act fast. Generous and good-hearted she might be, but the girl could stir up considerable of a temper when riled. Unless something happened to prevent it, the Countess stood a chance of being jumped and hand-scalped by a girl who could claim considerable ability in that line. Nor did the danger end there, for the other two men showed signs of taking cards in the game. So

Mark yelled his warning and sprang forward.

Landing on the undamaged trail before the group, Mark shot out a hand to take hold of Calamity by the pants seat and haul her behind him. Then he faced the men, legs apart, knees slightly bent and fingers spread over the butt of his right side Colt. Most likely his words meant little to the three men, but his attitude gave a warning. They had seen the speed with which he could draw and how accurately he placed his shots. Nor could they forget the strength he exhibited in clearing the rock out of their way. Such a man could not be ignored when he gave an order—at least not without a disproportionate amount of danger.

Instead of screaming to her men to help her, the Countess stared in Mark's direction. Slowly the almost animal rage left her features, to be replaced by a calculating gleam. She knew the nature of her men well enough to be aware that no mere bluff could make them hold back. If those three, specially chosen to be her escort, feared to tangle with the blond giant, he might be ideally suited to her needs. Forcing herself erect, she moved forward and ignored Calamity, who stood tense, watchful, ready to meet any further attack.

"There will be no further trouble, Mr. Counter," she said, after snapping an order in Italian to the men.

"I didn't know there'd been——," began Calamity.

"Choke off, Calam," Mark snapped. "Your boys shouldn't've tried to cut in, Countess."

"They are loyal servants and do not care to see a ——anybody lay hands on me in such a manner," the Countess replied.

Being very loyal to his employer, Mark could understand and sympathize with the trio for their actions. Calamity did not take such a lenient view.

"The next time he tries to take a rifle to me, I'll cut his hand off," she warned. "Let's get moving, Mark."

"I hoped that you and your—wife would accompany me to the Mission so that my husband could reward you for assisting me, Mr. Counter.''

"Him and his wife have to be in Robertstown tonight," Calamity stated.

"That's the living truth, ma'am," Mark agreed. "Only this isn't my wife. May I present Miss Martha Jane Canary."

"Better known as Calamity Jane," the red head explained.

"How quaint," purred the Countess. "Will you come, Mr. Counter?"

"I'd admire to, ma'am, but Calam's right. I do have to make Robertstown as soon as I can."

"Is your business so urgent that it won't wait a short time?" asked the Countess, struggling to hold her smile in the face of a refusal to blindly comply with her wishes.

"I told two good friends that I'd meet up with them in town," Mark explained. "One of them's my boss, too, and he wants to get back home as soon as he can."

For a moment the Countess did not reply, but digested the reply and saw in it an answer to her idea's chief snag.

"You do not own your own ranch?" she finally asked.

"No. I ride for the OD Connected."

"But surely you could do better than that?"

"Maybe," Mark answered, ignoring Calamity's angry snort.

"Why, my husband could use an experienced man such as you," the Countess went on. "If you came——."

"Like I said, ma'am," drawled Mark. "It can't be done."

"We would pay top wages——."

"That doesn't come into it," Mark said shortly. In the West one did not try to hire another spread's hands unless deliberately intending offence. Of course the

Countess might not know of the range convention. "Reckon I've no ambition, I don't want to change my boss."

In the face of such a flat statement the Countess could do nothing and realised further insistence might cause offence. Even if she called upon her men to enforce her wishes, it was doubtful whether they could do anything, or be willing to risk facing the blond giant. With an effort she held her temper and looked away from Mark, her eyes going to the ruined portion of the trail.

"It would appear that you are going to be late in joining your friends anyway," she remarked.

"How come, ma'am?" asked Mark.

"My horse refused to go across there."

"That was 'cause you——," Calamity began, but Mark interrupted before she completed her caustic comments on the Countess' ability as a horse-handler.

"We'll see what we can do," he said. "Let's get our horses, Calam."

While walking to their waiting mounts, Mark studied the three men. Sullen scowls met his gaze and the man who had tried to draw his rifle stood nursing a pain-throbbing hand. Mark knew too much about the Latin temperament to believe the incident forgotten. That surly cuss would be looking for a chance to avenge the blow given by Calamity. It might be unwise to trust the three, and that one particularly, too far; although they seemed obedient enough to the Countess' orders.

Calamity also examined the three men and her thoughts almost mirrored Mark's on reading the hate in her victim's eyes. Taking her buckskin's reins, she threw a glance in the blond giant's direction.

"I'll try first," she suggested.

Prudence dictated that only one horse at a time was on the narrow stretch of the trail. Horses could be difficult to handle under such conditions and one might easily decide half way over to back away instead of going forward. So Mark realised that he and Calamity could make the crossing singly while the other remained and watched the trio without their suspicions becoming too obvious.

Behaving much as had the Countess' dun, Calamity's buckskin at first followed obediently. On drawing close to the narrow section, the buckskin slowed down. Calamity drew gently on the reins, giving out a string of low-spoken profanity to which her mount had become accustomed. Normally the buckskin would have obeyed the reins, but it stood firm, with braced forelegs, refusing to go closer to that sudden drop. The Countess let out a short burst of mocking laughter.

"It seems that you can do no better than I!" she called.

"At least I've more sense than to try to whip the hoss across," Calamity replied, holding down her temper. "Have a go with your bloodbay, Mark."

Possibly the dun's fright had warned the other horses of danger. Whatever the reason, Mark's bloodbay stallion also refused to make the crossing. That told both Mark and Calamity they must adopt other tactics. The big horse possessed a steady nature and could be relied on not to spook under normal conditions, so its refusal meant that none of the other horses would go over.

Biting her lip, the Countess looked at the gap and contemplated the delay going right around the Wapiti Hills would cause. Yet no solution presented itself to her and she knew the three hired men lacked the necessary knowledge to supply an answer. If two such experienced horse-handlers as Mark and Calamity failed to lead their horses over the narrow stretch, the Countess' men were unlikely to meet with more success.

"We must all go around then," she said.

"Well now," drawled Mark, throwing a grin at Calamity. "I wouldn't say so."

"Or me," the red head agreed, reaching up to unfasten the bandana around her throat. "Shall I make a start, or will you?"

"How steady's that buckskin?"

"Good as any I've ever handled," Calamity replied. "Only I've never tried him on anything like this."

"It'd best be me then," Mark stated. "We can't take a chance on the first one refusing. Loan me your bandana."

"You tear it and I'll take a new one out of your hide," the girl warned.

Taking the bandana, Mark fastened it around the bay's face so as to cover the eyes. Having been treated in such a manner before, the stallion stood still and caused no fuss. Nor did it hesitate to follow him after he unfastened the pack pony from his saddle and walked towards the narrow area of the trail. Holding the reins short, Mark kept himself between the bloodbay and the edge as they moved on to the three foot wide section. One slip over the edge and he might not be able to halt himself; certainly could not happen the horse came over after him. So Mark did not rush things, but concentrated on leading the horse in a continuous walk. Panic now, a refusal by the big horse to follow, would mean complete failure if nothing worse.

At last Mark found himself on the wide trail and led his horse well clear of the narrow section before removing its blindfold. Turning, he looked back to the others.

"Send one of your men across to hold him, ma'am," he called.

"Carl!" snapped the Countess and gave an order in Italian.

After the man arrived and took the bloodbay's reins, Mark rejoined the remainder of the party. As he expected, Calamity held out her hand towards him.

"I'll go next," she said. Anybody who knew Calamity would expect her to insist on taking her own horse over the dangerous section.

Fixing the blindfold, Calamity led her buckskin forward. While always liking to grandstand a mite, Calamity knew better than take fool chances at such a time.

She found no difficulty in leading the horse over, but knew things might not be so easy with the rest of the animals.

"We'll leave your dun until last," Mark told the Countess as he prepared to blindfold the pack horse.

"And may I ask why?" she demanded, a hint of indignation in her voice.

"To give it a chance to settle down," the Texan explained. "When it sees the others go over, it'll be less likely to spook."

Being selected for docility, tractability, and a fair amount of sure-footedness, the pack pony gave no trouble at either being blindfolded or led across the gap. Which left the horses belonging to the Countess' party. Taking them over did not, as Calamity expected, prove so easy. The two men's mounts lacked confidence due to bad handling and showed reluctance to have the bandana tied over their eyes. Nor did the first horse follow easily with its vision obliterated, giving Mark a few bad moments before reaching the far side of the narrow stretch. However he made the crossing and returned for the second of the horses.

"Go ahead, Mark," Calamity said. "I'd best get the dun used to being under a blindfold before we try taking it."

"It'd be best," he agreed.

"I'll need a bandana, Mrs. Countess," Calamity remarked, turning to the blonde for the first time since starting the crossings.

"My handkerchief would not be large enough," the Countess replied. "Luigi will give you his."

Luigi proved to be the man who caught Calamity's whip earlier, but he raised no objections to handing over his bandana. Obtaining the bandana came easier than fitting it into place, for the Countess' dun was high-spirited, nervous almost, in the face of a new kind of treatment. It said much for Calamity's ability as a horse-handler that she managed to calm the dun's objections and fit the bandana without needing help from Mark.

"Shall I take him, Calam?" asked Mark on his return.

"Nope. Leave it to me, he's used to me by now."

Despite her casual answer, Calamity felt a mite uneasy as she brought the dun forward. The horse did not lead as easily as the others, stepping reluctantly and hesitantly in Calamity's tracks.

"Don't let him bump into the side, gal," Mark warned.

Even as he spoke, the dun's saddle struck the wall. Instantly Calamity's hold tightened and she steadied the horse, speaking gently and controlling its efforts to rear. Once the horse's feet clattered within an inch of the edge, but Calamity held firm and regained control to bring the dun to safety. Once on the wider section, she gave a long sigh and wiped the sweat from her face.

"That's done it," she breathed.

"It sure has," Mark agreed. "We'll make Robertstown on time yet, gal."

At Calamity's suggestion, the Countess had already crossed. Followed by her men, she advanced on the other two and her congratulations mingled with a spate of excited praises from the Italians. A thoughtful gleam came into the Countess' eyes as she watched her men's reactions to Mark. Turning on her heel, she looked to where the wine bottle stood at the side of the trail, set down as the women helped Mark to rise.

"May I repay you in some way for your help?" she asked, looking at Mark.

"Forget it," Calamity answered. "We'd've done it for anybody."

"Possibly, but I was the one who benefited," the Countess pointed out. "If you will not accept payment, surely you will help me finish the bottle of wine. My father once told me that nobody should leave a roast uneaten, or bottle unfinished."

"Why thanks, ma'am," Mark drawled. "I'd like that."

"Perhaps it would prove too strong for you?" purred the Countess to Calamity.

"Just pass the bottle and we'll see," Calamity replied hotly.

"Get your cup out of the bedroll, Calam," Mark suggested.

While Mark and Calamity collected the tin cups they carried, the Countess fetched the wine bottle. In doing so, she stood with her back to the others and took more time than the mere picking up merited. On returning, she poured two generous measures into the offered cups.

"Drink up," she smiled. "Good wine should be finished in one go, not sipped at and disturbed."

Accepting the implied challenge, Calamity up-ended her cup and poured the wine down her throat. Out of courtesy Mark did the same. Even as he drank, he wondered if the wine tasted different, decided it did and put it down to the raw state of his throat on the other occasion.

Suddenly a wave of dizziness hit Mark, causing him to stagger. The valley appeared to be whirling around, its floor rising and falling like the deck of a ship on a high sea. Before he could wonder at the change, his legs buckled under him and he went down, everything going black.

CHAPTER NINE

You Must Stay as a Guest, Mr. Counter

Glowing redly, the sun sank in the West and sent its rays through a small window into Mark's face. He blinked his eyes and sat up. For a moment the room spun around, then settled down to allow him the opportunity of studying it. Small, with undecorated stone walls, a wash stand, a stout door pierced by a covered peephole. The bed under him felt comfortable enough and his bedroll lay open at one side. Even as he swung himself erect, he realised that his gunbelt no longer hung at his waist. Exploratory fingers found the secret pocket in his waist belt still held the money placed there before leaving on the trip from the OD Connected. Only his gunbelt and the ammunition from his warbag appeared to be missing, for his Stetson hung on the end of the bed and boots, freshly cleaned, stood at the door.

Deciding to learn where he might be, Mark walked towards the window. Before he reached it, the door's lock clicked. Swinging around, Mark leapt forward, gripped the door's handle and jerked hard. A man clad in the sober black of a house-servant shot into the room and Mark caught him, swinging him effortlessly against the wall.

"Where am I?" the blond giant demanded.

Fear showed on the man's sallow face. "*Io non capisco, signore!*" he yelped.

Like most men born in the southern part of Texas, Mark spoke some Spanish; but the man had not used that language. However the meaning of the words was clear, the man did not understand. Seeing there would be no chance of learning anything from his captive, Mark set the man down and stepped from the room. He found himself in a corridor with other rooms on either side and a window which looked out over open range country. On reaching the window, Mark saw an open area, then a high stone wall and beyond it a pleasant valley with high, rocky sides.

"Ah, Mr. Counter," said a familiar voice from behind him. "You have recovered at last."

Turning, Mark found the Countess standing at the point where a flight of stairs opened on to the passage. She wore the same style clothing, although without the hat, and still had the quirt swinging from her wrist.

"What happened?" he asked. "Where am I?"

"You collapsed on the trail. It must have been a result of the strain you underwent moving that rock. So we brought you to my home."

"Where's Calam?"

"She rode on to Robertstown, to inform your friends."

Mark felt a touch of relief at the words, knowing Calamity to be capable of finding the town and so would inform Dusty of his reason for not arriving as promised. Then another thought hit Mark.

"My gunbelt's gone," he said.

"If you come this way, my husband will explain everything," the Countess replied and appeared to take his agreement for granted, for she turned and walked towards the head of the stairs.

Mark followed the woman downstairs to the ground floor. While going down, he studied the large entrance

hall, with closed doors leading off into various rooms.
There were a number of questions he wanted to ask, but
decided to wait until he saw the Countess' husband.
Leading the way, the Countess halted at a door and
knocked, then opened it.

"Our guest has recovered, Alberto," she said and
stood aside. "Come in, Mr Counter, please."

Walking by the woman, Mark entered a large, well-
furnished room with a barred window that looked out
on to the high-walled yard. Unless he missed his guess,
the bars had been fitted recently, certainly not when the
mission was first built. The large safe in the corner of
the room gave a hint of why the bars had been fitted.

After a quick glance around the room, Mark turned
his attention to its two male occupants. Seated behind a
large desk, Count Alberto Giovanni gazed back at the
blond giant and then swung his eyes in the direction of
his wife. Mark studied the man. Big, fat, lethargic, with
a soft-skinned face that held an expression of veiled
cruelty, the piggy eyes glinting calculatingly as he
looked from the Texan to his wife. He wore a silk robe
and cravat, expensive and built to his fit. When he
spoke, his voice sounded cultured and without trace of
an accent.

"Welcome, Mr. Counter," he said, returning his cold
eyes to the Texan's face. "Katherine has told me of your
indisposition, gained assisting her. May I offer you my
hospitality until you are fully recovered."

"I feel well enough now," Mark replied. "Reckon I'll
be riding on."

While speaking, Mark gave a long glance at the man
standing behind the Count's chair. No Italian that one,
but a type Mark knew all too well. Tanned, yet with
hands that showed no sign of hard work such as a
cowboy did, the man wore a frilly bosomed white shirt,
string tie, tight legged trousers and town boots. Around
his waist hung a gunbelt with a rose-wood handled

Civilian Peacemaker in a shaped, fast-draw holster. The tan of his face told that he spent time in the open, his clothes and weapon said plainly how he earned his pay. Before Mark could form any conclusion, the Count spoke again.

"But I couldn't hear of it. I have some medical knowledge so you may accept my judgment that it would be most unwise of you to attempt to make a long journey until you are fully recovered. You must stay until your friend returns from Robertstown with the doctor."

"I'll think about it," Mark promised. "Where are my guns?"

The tall gun-hand behind the Count stiffened slightly, although only trained eyes would have noticed the difference in him. Being trained, Mark saw it and guessed he would not approve of what he heard next.

"I have them locked away," the Count informed him. "You see, Mr. Counter, while you rendered my dear lady wife some assistance, I know nothing about you and circumstances force me never to allow strangers to wear weapons in my presence."

"I haven't shot a stranger in days," Mark drawled.

"Probably not. Yet I decline to take chances. No offence, Mr. Counter, but in the old country I incurred the enmity of the Mafia, a terrible criminal organization, and they have sworn to kill me."

"I'm not one of them,"

"The Mafia has never hesitated to hire outside aid if they failed," the Count pointed out. "Again, no offence, but you must see my position: and I give you my word that your arms will be returned when you leave."

Although Mark did not care to be regarded as untrustworthy, he could see the Count's point of view. Besides, with that deadly cuss standing out of reaching distance and wearing a gun, Mark could not take violent objection to his host's wishes.

"You may as well give them to me, I'll be going," he said.

"But no," objected the Count. "You must stay as a guest, Mr. Counter. I insist that you do. I could not have you leave and perhaps collapse on the trail."

"All right," Mark drawled, knowing he could not resist in the face of an armed and obviously very competent paid gun fighter. "How about my horse?"

"Mr. Baton here attended to it," the Count replied, giving his first indication of the gun-hand's presence.

"I off-saddled him and turned him loose down the valley," Barton said. "Likely couldn't find him afore dark."

"Then you must stay at least until morning," smiled the Countess.

"Feel free to go anywhere in the house, Mr. Counter," the Count went on. "Of course much of it is locked as the flooring is unsafe."

"How about outside?" asked Mark.

"If you wish to go out, Mr. Barton will accompany you. I have loyal servants, Mr. Counter, very loyal. They are nervous and under orders to prevent anybody entering or leaving without my permission."

"There are certain parts of the grounds into which you must not g——," the Countess began.

At that moment the door of the room opened and a tall, burly man entered.

"Boss," he said. "The muckers saw snow and're getting scared of a run."

"Wait!" the Count barked. "My dear, show Mr. Counter around."

Clearly the Count did not want Mark to hear any more of the newcomer's news. Mark had turned at the man's entrance and been surprised at what he saw. The very last person Mark expected to meet in this place was a hard-rock underground miner and yet, unless his clothes and speech lied, there stood one. A hard-fisted gang boss, too, or Mark did not know the type.

Even as that thought came, Mark saw something which wiped it from his head. A long bull whip hung coiled over the back of a chair by the door. Not just an ordinary whip. Mark had seen it often enough to recognise it as that plaited specially for Calamity Jane. Only with an effort did he prevent his surprise and anxiety showing, or avoid allowing the others to notice that he saw the whip. Even if he had not felt it before, he now knew something to be bad wrong. Calamity would never part with her whip and was more likely to leave her pants than the long-lashed tool of her profession.

"Come with me, Mr. Counter," said the Countess.

Seething with anxiety for Calamity's safety, Mark followed the woman from the room. It seemed that the miner's business had a certain urgency, for even as the door started to close, Mark heard him start speaking again.

"They're getting restless again, Count——."

"That is Mr. Whales," the Countess remarked. "He is—employed to rebuild the place. I can't understand half he says."

Although he did not let on, Mark *had* understood. During the time he helped Dusty Fog tame a wild Montana town,* Mark came across many miners and learned something of their talk. "Muckers" had been a term for the underground workers. Unless Mark's memory failed him, "snow" meant a trickle of fine earth from the roof of an underground passage and might herald a "run", cave-in. Which meant that Whales was not employed to rebuild the mission.

A door at the end of the passage flew open and a man emerged. Blood trickled down his forehead, but Mark recognised him as the member of the Countess' escort who felt Calamity's whip back on the trail. Quickly the

*Told in QUIET TOWN by J. T. Edson.

man slammed the door, but not before Mark had heard a distant, feminine yelling.

Leaving Mark, the Countess advanced on the man and angry words spat from her. The man looked sheepish and slunk away, passing Mark with only a single glowering scowl.

"A—mishap in the kitchen," said the Countess returning to Mark's side. "We have a rather hot-blooded and temperamental cook."

"Sounds that way," lied Mark, for the voice had sounded remarkably like that of a very angry Calamity Jane. "How's about going in the kitchen and seeing what's riling her?"

"Later. She doesn't like visitors and when she's in that mood even I am *persona non grata*. Come upstairs, I wish to show you the dining hall. As you see, we have made few improvements to the property as yet. Later we hope to have it furnished and decorated in the manner to which we are accustomed."

As she talked, the Countess led Mark up the wide flight of stairs to the first floor. Clearly she wanted to take his thoughts from the incident just witnessed. Knowing he could do nothing at that moment, and that showing his hand would ruin any chances later, Mark allowed himself to be steered up the stairs. At the top, he walked along the passage and looked out of the window. From there he could see over the wall and looked along a valley. High ragged walls rose up on each side, already gloomy with the setting sun. Far from the house horses grazed, but too far for him to be able to locate his bloodbay.

"A pleasant view," the Countess said. "Of course you can't see the wall at the other end right now."

"How do you get out," asked Mark, conscious of her closeness and feeling her hand on his sleeve.

"Through the front gate," she replied. "You can see it from the dining hall. Come, I'll show you."

Turning from the window, Mark followed the woman into the central set of doors. Beyond them he found a long room scattered with small tables and cushions instead of chairs, and a large, comfortable divan in the center. Ignoring the Countess' glances at the divan, Mark walked across to where a large window opened on to a balcony. He leaned on the protective wall of the balcony and looked around him. Down below lay an open piece of ground with a lean-to built against the outside wall. A further wall, as high as that surrounding the building, separated the part into which Mark looked from an open square before the main doors. On the far side of the square, a couple of wagons stood without their teams. Another wall, with a door in it, lay beyond the wagons, for no reason that Mark could see. Stretching from the square, a straight trail ran down a valley and joined a pass in the Wapiti Hills some half a mile away. Mark saw a couple of rifle-armed men on either side of the valley, positioned so as to cover its entrance. Any rider or party trying to force its way to the house would have to run the gauntlet of the guards' cross-fire in the open.

"Your husband doesn't believe in taking any chances," he commented to the woman as she followed him.

"He doesn't," she agreed, laying her hand once more on Mark's sleeve. "Each man has two rifles and is a good shot, so it would be inadvisable for anyone to enter—or to leave—without permission."

"Sure looks that way," Mark drawled.

"My husband fears for his life——"

"What the hell!" interrupted Mark, staring down at a couple of animals which emerged from the lean-to. "They're lions!"

"Alberto bought them after the male killed its trainer at a circus we attended in Santa Fe," the Countess explained. "They're his pets."

"Some pets," growled Mark, staring at the black-manned male and its slightly smaller, mane-less consort.

"They have their uses," the Countess smiled. "By the way, their compound stretches all the way around the building, except for the square. We find difficulty in feeding them, so it would not do to walk out among them."

"How many of those damned critters have you?"

"Three. The lion and two lionesses. We did have four, but a lioness escaped some days ago. It must have slipped out of the valley, for we can't find it."

"That'll please the ranchers outside the hills, happen it gets among their stock." Mark commented. "Mountain lions are bad enough, and they're not half one of those lionesses' size."

"Let's go inside," the Countess suggested. "We sometimes feed the lions from up here and our presence disturbs them."

Already the two animals from the lean-to circled beneath the window and their guttural growling brought the other lioness loping around the side of the building. Mark wondered what prompted the Count to buy such strange pets.

"Can't say as how I'd like to have them roaming outside my house," he said. "Happen somebody walked out of the house——"

"We keep the downstairs doors locked and windows barred," the Countess replied and walked back into the room.

Mark threw a final glance around him, trying to estimate his chances of getting from the house to his horse and then out of the valley. To do so meant crossing the open square, which probably had a guard at night. Until seeing the lions he had thought of using some other exit. It would be impossible if the Countess spoke the truth. More than ever Mark wondered what he found himself mixed up with. The presence of the miner and hints at working underground, and the guards gave him a possible answer. Yet secret mining did not account for why he and Calamity had been drugged, as he now felt sure they had, and brought to the mission.

Suddenly the Countess was up close to him, her arms slipping about him, the right around his neck and left creeping up his back as she tried to draw his face down to her own.

"Mark!" she gasped. "Kiss me, Mark!"

"What about your husband?" he asked.

"*Him!*" disgust showed in the woman's voice. "You saw him. Fat, bloated. I need a man, Mark. A man like you."

Again she moved closer, standing on her very toes and managing to reach the blond giant's lips with her own. Her mouth felt hot, passionate; and her body rode nearer, the bust forcing against him. Under different circumstances Mark might have welcomed such attentions, for he sensed that the Countess could handle her end at love-making. Mark was no prude and enjoyed women's company; but he drew the line at making love to a man's wife while a guest under his roof.

Feeling Mark's lack of response, the Countess moved away and looked long at him. At that moment Mark remembered Calamity was a prisoner in the house, confined in the cellar or he missed his guess. The Countess might be a key to rescuing Calamity, so he could not chance antagonising her too far.

"You don't like me," she hissed.

"I like you fine," drawled Mark. "Only I don't figure your husband'd be too happy about us getting friendly."

"You aren't afraid of him," she stated.

"Maybe not. But he does have a tolerable amount of help he can call on."

"I can handle most of them."

Suddenly she whisked further away from him and her face took on an expression of bored innocence. The main doors opened to admit the Count followed by Baton.

"Here you are, Katherine," the Count said. "We are giving a small dinner and entertainment tonight. Do you think Mr. Counter will enjoy it?"

"I believe he might," the woman replied. "But our supplies are low, can we manage it?"

"We have t——," began the Count, then threw a glance at Mark. "Of course we can, my dear. Come along and help me make arrangements."

"How about our guest?"

"Possibly Mr. Barton would care to entertain him until time for dinner."

"Sure, Boss," Baton answered.

"I've just been admiring your pets," Mark drawled, jerking his head towards the window.

"Charming creatures," the Count replied. "Do you know, Mr. Counter, that the ancient Romans used to drop human beings to their lions for sport and diversion during their feasts?"

"Me, I'd rather play poker," Mark answered.

"So, I suppose, would the people selected to be fed to the lions," said the Count and, taking his wife's arm, left the room.

"What do you make of 'em?" asked Baton.

"They seem all right, even if he has a lousy sense of humor," Mark replied. "Is he really that scared of those Italian jaspers coming after him?"

"Try making a wrong move and you'll find out," warned the gun-hand. "Those fellers he brought from Italy'd kill you without thinking twice about it."

"How about you?"

"I do what I'm paid to do."

"What'd that be?" drawled Mark.

"Let's say I'm his segundo," Baton replied. "Which

same, I'm wondering why she brought you here.''

"I took sick on the trail," Mark reminded him.

"That's what I heard," said Baton. "You're *the* Mark Counter, Dusty Fog's right bower, aren't you?"

"So they tell me," Mark replied.

Baton lapsed into silence and looked thoughtful. Then he gave a shrug and suggested that he showed Mark the rest of the building while the house staff prepared the room for the dinner.

"How about looking around the kitchen?" asked Mark.

"The cook's a mite-busy right now."

"And she don't take to having visitors?"

"She?" Baton repleated, sounding puzzled. "Our cook's a man."

"Reckon I must have made a mistake then," Mark said. "Let's take that stroll, shall we?"

CHAPTER TEN

They're Giving the Thumbs Down
For You, Mr. Counter

There had been a time when Mark Counter would have taken the first opportunity to jump Baton, gain possession of his gun and then rely on luck to make his escape. Years of riding with Dusty Fog taught him wisdom and to think before acting. So instead of going off half-cocked, the blond giant waited and watched, wanting to learn all he could before making his move.

Mark had plenty of chances to look over the situation. Accompanied by Baton, he strolled around such parts of the house as were not locked and even took a look around outside. Clearly escape would not be easy. In addition to the four-man guard at the far end of the gorge leading to the building, a further quartet stood by on the porch. From what Mark could see, the men took their duties seriously. There were Italians, the same cold-eyed kind who had accompanied the Countess and who Baton claimed to be absolutely loyal to their employer.

"It's time we went up to the diningroom," Baton remarked, as they stood in the darkness and looked along the gorge.

In the background, beyond the wall, the lion let out a

roar and Mark looked at the other man. "He sounds hungry."

"Likely he'll get fed tonight," Baton replied, and threw a glance up to the lighted windows above them. "Let's get in. I reckon you'll find the Count's dinners interesting."

Followed by Baton, Mark returned to the entrance hall. Without even a glance at the door which he felt led to where Calamity Jane was held a prisoner, Mark walked upstairs. He believed that the others did not know his suspicions and wanted it kept that way as long as possible.

Things had apparently been moving fast since Mark left the diningroom. At one side of the main doors, two cooks stood by a long, food-loaded table and piled up generous helpings on to plates. On the other side of the door another man presided over a table bearing numerous bottles and glasses. Scattered about the room, lounging at ease on the various cushions, men took their ease. Not Italians, but Bohunks, mid-Europeans, of the sort one saw working underground in gold-mining towns. Whales sat at one side of the divan on which sprawled the Count who accepted a drink from a glass held by a good-looking girl.

Not only the Count received such attentions. Some dozen girls served the men with food and drinks. While the girls were such that they might have been found in any good class saloon, Mark had never seen so daring costumes; not even at the height of the feud between Freddie Woods and Buffalo Kate, rival saloon owners in Mulrooney, Kansas.* Until, in the interests of keeping the peace, Dusty stopped the feud, both women dressed their employees in progressively more *risque* costumes, but neither reached the standard of the girls in the Count's diningroom. Each girl wore a flowing

*Told in THE TROUBLE BUSTERS by J. T. Edson.

dress of flimsy material and little else, if the one who approached Mark and Baton was anything to go on.

"Hey, Bat honey," she greeted. "Who's your friend?"

"Call him 'Mark'," Baton replied.

"Ah, Mr. Counter!" called the Count. "Come over and join me, sir." He waved a hand to one of the cushion seats as Mark walked over. "Sit down. Wine and food for Mr. Counter, Doris. And how do you like my way of dining, Mr. Counter?"

"It beats anything we have at the OD Connected," Mark admitted, watching the girl who greeted Baton hurry across to the table. "Only I don't reckon Ole Devil Hardin'd go for it."

Nor would Dusty's cousin, the beautiful and talented Betty Hardin, if it came to a point, Mark told himself, and her word was law around the OD Connected.

"I find that this kind of thing has a soothing effect upon my workers," the Count remarked. "When they become restless, an orgy shows them the benefits of remaining in my employ."

"That's smart thinking," Mark replied, guessing that such an answer would gain him information that might be of use in escaping. One could never know too much about the enemy.

"Not original, I'm afraid," the Count sighed. "Although my family can trace itself back to the highest born of Rome. The Caesars knew of such things before the birth of Christ. That was why they organised the circuses. In my own small way I try to emulate them."

In his boyhood, Mark received a fair education and seemed to recall that the circuses of ancient Rome had different attractions to those presented by the tent shows which occasionally visited Texas.

His thoughts on the matter died down as another girl entered, by far the best-looking of them all. Tall, with blonde hair framing a sultry, beautiful face, she had a body that was all any man could desire in a woman, and knew it. Clearly she did not merely come in, but made an entrance. Pausing until every male eye went to her, she started to advance slowly across the room. Yet, although they stared at her and did not hesitate to maul any of the other girls, not one of the men offered to lay a hand on the blonde.

"Sheila, my dear," said the Count, beaming at the girl. "Come and meet my new guest."

Such had been the interest in the gorgeous blonde that the Countess came in unnoticed by another door. Apart from the hat, she wore the same clothes as during her first meeting with Mark and the quirt still hung at her right wrist. Walking forward without a glance at the surrounding scene, the Countess passed in front of Sheila as if the blonde did not exist. Not quite though, for in passing the Countess threw a mocking, challenging look in Sheila's direction.

"Fetch me a drink," the Countess ordered.

Sheila's lips drew into a tight line and she seemed on the verge of refusing. Then slowly her eyes went down to the Countess' riding boots, comparing them with her own light slippers, and from there to the quirt now held in the other's hand, tapping lightly against her thigh. Without a word, Sheila turned and walked away in the direction of the drinks table.

"I intended to ask Sheila to serve Mr. Counter, my dear," the Count said. "As an honored guest, he deserves the best."

"But what of——?" the Countess began.

Cutting off her words in a flow of Italian, the Count made some comment which brought first a frown, then a calculating gleam to the Countess' face. Mark did not know what she aimed to say, but her husband appeared to have changed her mind. After Sheila returned with the drink and passed it over accompanied by a scowl, the Countess raised no objections to her husband's suggestion that she served Mark. Nor did the blonde appear averse to doing so.

"Will you eat, or drink first, Mr. Counter?" asked the Count. "Just tell Sheila and she will fetch you anything you need."

"It'll be a pleasure," purred Sheila, dropping to the cushion at Mark's side. Then she looked across the room in a half-scared manner. "*Il Bruto!*" she gasped.

"*Il Bruto!*" the words were repeated, passing around the room as its occupants stared to and from Mark and a newcomer who stood at the main doors.

Following the direction of the gazes, Mark saw a big man at the door. At least as tall as the blond giant and maybe heavier, the newcomer wore a sleeveless vest and no shirt, showing off his powerful muscular development. His head had been shaved, or was naturally hairless, and he possessed the most ugly, vicious face Mark had ever seen.

For a moment the man called *Il Bruto* stood glaring around as if looking for somebody. Then his eyes came to rest on Sheila as she sat at Mark's side. Letting out a low snort, *Il Bruto* stalked across the floor. A silence that could almost be felt dropped on the room. Sheila let out a low whine of fear as the huge man came to a halt and reached down to grip her wrist. With an effortless gesture, *Il Bruto* started to drag the girl to her feet.

Mark's southern-trained chivalry caused him to start to rise. Before the Texan could do more than lift his rump from the cushion, *Il Bruto* swung a backhand blow which caught him in the face, lifted him partially erect and flung him backwards. Mark felt his legs strike the divan and he went over it. Although his horseman's reflexes helped him break the fall, he still crashed down hard. Springing forward, having thrust Sheila aside, *Il Bruto* bent over, laid hold of Mark's shirt front, dragged him erect and hurled him across the room. Such was the bald man's strength that Mark shot across the room and crashed into the wall. By the time he reached it, however, Mark managed to twist so that his shoulder struck the hard rock instead of him smashing face-first into it.

Expecting no trouble, *Il Bruto* advanced without taking precautions. He learned the error of his ways when Mark pivoted around and smashed a backhand blow which jerked his head around, then ripped a punch across to swing it in the other direction. The force of the blows rocked the bulk of *Il Bruto* backwards.

Letting out a snarl of rage, *Il Bruto* sprang forward with big hands reaching to clamp hold of the big Texan. Always before *Il Bruto's* strength and weight gave him an advantage over his opponents. For the first time he found himself facing a man at least as strong, if not quite as heavy, and one fully conversant with all kinds of fighting. Mark went under a raking blow at his head and ripped a hard blow into the other man's gut, feeling the hard solidity of it. Although *Il Bruto* grunted, he did not fall back. Side-stepping the other's advance, Mark smashed a blow to the side of the bald head and *Il Bruto* shot on to hit the wall.

While waiting for *Il Bruto* to turn, Mark threw a quick glance at the Count and Countess. One look told him that they did not intend to have the fight stopped. Cool, calculating interest showed on the Countess' thin face and the expression of sadistic lust told Mark all he needed to know about her husband. The Count had known what to expect when he told Sheila to attend to Mark, now he sat back watching the fight with evil, piggy eyes. The rest of the occupants of the room scattered, standing back against the walls and giving the fighters plenty of room.

Swinging away from the wall, *Il Bruto* charged again and Mark rammed a punch into his face. Normally such a blow would have halted the rush. It pulped *Il Bruto's* nose but did not stop his advance. Around lashed his

fist in a slow, awkward blow that landed with considerable power at the side of Mark's jaw and drove him
backwards. Following up with lumbering speed, the
bald man hurled another blow but Mark had regained
his balance. Throwing up his right hand, Mark deflected
the blow and hooked savagely at *Il Bruto's* body with
the left. Another punch lashed at Mark's head and he
ducked under it, coming up close, then backing off and
whipping three punches to the ugly, fury-contorted
face. Spitting blood, *Il Bruto* bored in again. He still
had not realised the danger and did not change from his
usual fighting tactics.

Against a man of Mark's capabilities such tactics
were dangerous to their user. Yet such was the brute
strength of *Il Bruto* that he gave the blond giant the
hardest fight of his life. For twenty minutes it raged
around the room watched by a first noisy, then silent
crowd.

A savage right caught Mark in the stomach and
rocked him backwards, then a left landed on his face,
sending him crashing into the wall. Following Mark up,
Il Bruto trapped his left arm, twisting it around behind
Mark's back in a hammerlock. Savagely the bald man
twisted at the arm, his two hands needed to fight the
Texan's strength. Then he started to swing Mark
towards the open window which led to the balcony.
Muttering curses from his bloody lips, *Il Bruto* began to
move Mark in the direction of the balcony.

Excitement and anticipation came to every face as the
watchers saw what *Il Bruto* aimed to do. Suddenly Mark
remembered the lions and realised his assailant's intention. More than that, he guessed such an end had come
to other fights. One look at the Count's face, drooling
almost as he made his way across the room, told Mark
he called the play correctly. Disappointment, rather
than concern, showed on the Countess' face as she
watched Mark being forced across the room.

Bracing his heels, Mark halted *il Bruto's* progress, but

the pain in his arm drove nausea into him and he knew he must escape from the hammerlock. Reaching up and back with his free hand, Mark tried to catch hold of the other man's head as the first move in freeing himself, but could gain no hold on that slippery, sweat-slicked dome. In his attempt to avoid the reaching fingers, *Il Bruto* pulled his head back and his body advanced closer to Mark. With the speed that he showed when drawing his Colts, Mark brought the arm down and smashed its elbow to the rear. It drove with battering-ram force full into *Il Bruto's* body, sent with all the weight Mark could muster. A croak left *Il Bruto's* lips as two ribs broke under the impact. His hands left Mark's arm and he stumbled back. Turning fast, Mark ripped up his good arm in a punch which exploded with all his strength under the other's jaw. *Il Bruto* lifted erect, spun around and crashed into the wall on the side already injured by Mark's elbow. A screech of pain burst from him and he collapsed, rolling in agony and as incapable of further effort as a back-broke rabbit.

Mark realised he had nothing further to fear and halted in his tracks. All around him, the occupants of the room began to yell cheers. A look of baffled rage crossed the Count's face, then he smiled although it did not reach his eyes. Looking around him, he raised a hand.

"Well?" he asked, as silence fell.

Gasping for breath, half-blinded by sweat, Mark stood staring as the men and women raised their hands with the fist clenched and thumbs directed towards the floor.

"They're giving the thumbs down for you, Mr. Counter," the Count called, waving a hand towards the painfully moving shape of *Il Bruto*. "Finish him off."

"He's finished," Mark replied.

"But not to our satisfaction," declared the Count, and snapped his fingers. Four of the men moved forward, each taking hold of one of *Il Bruto's* limbs.

Raising the man, they carried him towards the open windows. Badly hurt though he was, *Il Bruto* realised what they meant to do and tried to struggle free. Suddenly, shockingly, Mark realised what the four intended and he started to move in their direction.

"My hero!" screeched Sheila, taking a line so often heard in the melodramatic plays of the period as she threw herself forward into Mark's arms.

At the same moment Baton lunged before Mark, a drawn Colt in his hand. "Hold back, man," the gun-hand warned. "It's for your own sake. They'd throw you over as well if you interfered."

"You can't let them——!" Mark began, trying to free himself from Sheila's clinging grasp long enough to take some action against Baton.

"They've seen *Il Bruto* throw three men over," replied Baton.

With a surging heave, the four men swung *Il Bruto's* body up and out, sending it over the veranda wall. A scream rang out, followed by the thud of his body as it landed. Then came a rushing sound, another hideous screech almost drowned by a snarling roar. Excited comment rose from the men and women who crowded on to the balcony or looked down from the room's other windows, laughter, chatter and pointing fingers coming as if they watched nothing more than the feeding of horse-meat to the caged animals in a zoological gardens.

"It's over," Baton said, and holstered his Colt.

"Let's go take a look, Mark," suggested Sheila.

Mark shook his head. Although used to violence and sudden death, the sight just witnessed sickened him and more than ever he wondered just what kind of folk he found himself among. The Countess stood by the window, her face alight with an expression of interest and savage delight as bad, if not worse, than that showed by the other on-lookers.

"Your poor face," Sheila gasped suddenly. "No

wonder you don't want to go look just now. You must be all tuckered out. Come and sit down."

"To the victor the spoils, I see, Mr. Counter," called the Count, turning from the window and looking to where Mark sat on the divan with Sheila bathing his face from a bowl of water and using a piece ripped off her skirt.

Already the other members of the party started to turn from the window and none showed enmity towards Mark. Every man present had lived in fear of *Il Bruto*, who outworked them; and none could tell when the bald man might pick a fight with him, ending in the fate just meted out.

Praise in several mid-European languages and broken English mingled with toasts drunk to Mark and the pace of the party began to speed up. Never had the blond giant seen such flagrant debauchery. The happenings in that room made the wildest end-of-drive celebrations seem as harmless as a church quilting-party. Yet behind it all Mark saw a definite purpose. Contriving to drink sparingly, he kept his eyes and ears open.

"Pour it down, boys," exhorted Whales, who like the Count and Baton drank little. "It'll be your last chance."

Listening to the words, Mark saw concern show on several of the muckers' faces. One of them, with a girl perched on his knee and a wine bottle in hand, glared at the gang boss.

"How you mean, last chance? Ain't there going to be no more parties like this then?"

"Sure there are. You know the Count likes giving 'em. Only I thought you bunch didn't like working for him."

"I never said I don't like," the mucker protested, and several others raised their voices in agreement.

"Some of you said the roof wasn't safe," the Count pointed out. "I do not wish to employ men who can't trust me to look after their welfare.''

"We trust you," stated another of the muckers, caressing the hips of a girl who held a large glass of wine for him. "I never seen any snow come down."

Again the chorus of agreement rolled around the room, including from the two men who first saw the trickle of fine earth running from a crack in the tunnel roof and gave the alarm.

"We show you in the morning," promised one of the pair. "We go down and dig like never before."

"We sure will," chorused the rest, and the girls screeched their delight.

"A dance, Sheila!" called the Countess, and the others took up the shout.

Rising reluctantly, Sheila moved into the center of the floor and began a sinuous writhing dance which showed off every inch of her splendid figure. Even in his present condition, Mark could not help staring at the sight. No dance he had ever seen equalled that exhibition. Any saloonkeeper or theatre manager trying to duplicate it would be closed instantly by the local law.

"You have won quite a prize, Mr. Counter," the Count purred lounging on the divan while Mark sat once more on a cushion.

"Looks that way," Mark agreed. "Reckon I'll go to bed, I'm a mite tuckered out one way and another."

"You must wait and allow Sheila to light you there," the Count objected, directing a glance at his wife.

"Perhaps Mr. Counter only wants to relax, Alberto," she put in.

"And what is more relaxing than Sheila," the Count replied, with a bawl of laughter.

Without another word, the Countess rose and walked from the room. Sheila finished the dance by flopping into Mark's lap, coiling her arms round his neck and kissing him.

"Mr. Counter is tired, my dear," the Count told her.

"Will you show him the way to his room?"

"Will I?" she replied eagerly. "Let's go, Mark honey."

Rising, Mark slipped an arm around Sheila's waist and left the room with her, followed by the admiring cheers of the celebrating miners. On the way to his room, Mark had to pass the main staircase and looked down at the entrance hall. A couple of Italians sat by the main doors, resting rifles on their knees. Despite the celebrations upstairs, they showed every sign of being awake and soberly alert. Maybe later, after the noise of the party had died down, they would relax and give him his chance.

"What's this?" Mark asked, looking at the house-servant he had seen just after recovering.

The man stood holding a tray on which stood two glasses. Offering the tray, he said something Mark could not understand.

"Well, I'll be——!" Sheila said, taking one glass. "This's the first time that scraggy bitch ever offered me a drink."

"Who?" asked Mark, although he could guess.

"The Countess. That lousy, skinny cat-house cull's sent us some of their fancy wine."

"You sound like you don't like her," Mark drawled.

"I hate her guts. One day I'm going to get her when she's not wearing those boots or toting the quirt, then I'm going to snatch her bald-headed."

"Maybe the Count wouldn't go for that," warned Mark, opening the door.

"The hell he won't!" spat Sheila. "I've seen how he looks at me, only he's scared of her. Once I've fixed her wagon, it'll be me who runs things here."

"Let's drink to that," drawled Mark, scooping one glass from the offered tray and walking into the room.

Inside the room, Sheila walked forward and flopped on to the bed. "To us!" she said, raising her glass, then draining it.

Mark did not reply, or drink the toast. Remembering what happened the last time he tried one of the Countess' drinks, he decided to abstain. Fortunately Sheila had already drunk enough not to notice his lapse of manners. Flinging her glass across the room, she rolled on to her back on the bed, throwing out her arms invitingly. Mark walked forward and sat on the edge of the bed, tossing the contents of his glass underneath it before copying the girl's disposal method. Then he leaned forward and kissed her.

"Tha's nice," she sighed, twining her arms around his neck. "I—I—tired—feel—feel——."

The arms went limp and Mark pulled himself free, looking down at Sheila. A sound outside the door caught his ear and he stretched out on the bed alongside the girl, feigning sleep. Hinges creaked and the door opened. Mark remained still, trying to match the girl at his side's steady breathing and listening to the soft footsteps approaching.

Reaching the bed, the Countess gripped Mark's shoulder and rolled him on to his back. Nothing about him gave the slightest hint that he was awake and, after looking at him, the Countess reached across his still frame. She gripped Sheila, sinking savage fingers into the girl's cheeks and shaking the blonde head from side to side viciously. Only a dull moan left Sheila's lips and the Countess let loose, allowing the girl's head to flop back on to the pillow. Nodding in satisfaction, the Countess leaned forward and kissed Mark's unresponsive lips, then she straightened up.

"That'll hold you until morning," she said with a hint of satisfaction, and walked out of the room, closing the door.

CHAPTER ELEVEN

We Can't Both Make it Out of Here

Not until half an hour after the sounds of distant revelry died away did Mark rise from the bed. Either the Countess felt confident that the drugged drink would hold him until morning, or believed that he suspected nothing and could be trusted not to make trouble. Whatever the reason, she had not locked the door and it opened to Mark's pull. Following his usual practice when staying indoors, Mark had donned his moccasins instead of the riding boots; for which he felt grateful as they offered the opportunity to move silently.

Finding nobody in the darkened passage, Mark moved silently along it towards the stairs. On peering cautiously around, he saw Baton standing talking before the open door to the inside and porch guards. Even as Mark watched, the gun-hand pointed off into the darkness and the quartet trooped away through the door. Turning, Baton passed through the circle of light thrown by the lamp over the main door and walked in the direction of the Count's study, knocked and entered.

Quickly, but without undue noise, Mark went down the stairs. He kept to the shadows as much as possible

and paused at the bottom. To reach the door beyond
which he suspected Calamity was held prisoner, Mark
had to pass the study. Voices reached his ears as he went
by the door and he halted in the hope that he might
learn something of use to his escape bid.

"We ought to have got that wagon off earlier,"
Baton was saying.

"With the muckers acting up, we couldn't spare any
of the guards to go," the Count replied. "And I always
like a full strength guard around during one of our
entertainments. It's safer that way."

"If they leave as soon as the wagon's ready, they'll
make Robertstown this afternoon," the Countess went
on. "That way, we'll have them back late tonight."

"I don't like using Robertstown so soon," protested
the Count.

"We have to," his wife told him. "There's no time to
send right around the Hills and we daren't put the men
on short rations."

"What're you fixing to do about the supplies now,
Count?" asked Baton. "If we suddenly start buying
them all in Robertstown, folks're going to want to know
what's going on. They'll figure we've more folks here
than we let on about."

"It's something we'll have to think about," the
Countess admitted.

"I said all along slow-elking wasn't the answer,"
Baton reminded the others.

"We had to have fresh meat in large quantities," the
Count pointed out. "And we couldn't buy it without
arousing suspicion."

"It still asked for touble," Baton answered. "So did
bringing Counter and that damned gal here."

"Why did you bring them, my dear?" purred the
Count.

"I *told* you," answered the Countess. "Some of the

things they said aroused my suspicions and made me wonder if they might not be hired to find out about us. So I drugged them and brought them here."

"I don't like it," insisted Baton.

"M—Mr. Counter suspects nothing and believes the girl has gone to Robertstown. When he learns different, her presence makes her an ideal hostage," replied the Countess. "We'll send Luigi and Carolo as guards with Benito driving."

"Are you going along, my dear?"

"Not this time, Alberto. We can rely on them and my presence might lead to questions."

"All right then," Baton said. "I'll go tell them."

"You may as well wait until I make out the list," the Countess told him.

Mark knew he must waste no more time. If he failed to make the most of the present opportunity, another might not present itself. Leaving the study door, he walked along the passage to where the man emerged earlier that day. A key stuck out of the lock and Mark turned it, opening the door. Inside he could see nothing, so after closing the door he lit a match. A short flight of stone steps led down into a cellar. Close at hand a lamp rested on a small shelf. Mark took the lamp, finding it to hold fuel, and lit it. While going down the stairs, he examined his surroundings. The cellar appeared to be used for a store, with piles of empty sacks and boxes scattered around. Of the three doors, only one caught Mark's eye. It had a barred grill at the upper end and a hinged section on the bottom, while a heavy bolt, newly fitted, fastened it.

"Calam!" he whispered, approaching the door.

"Mark!"

Despite the relief she must feel, Calamity did not panic and spoke in a low, vibrant hiss. Her face appeared at the grille, worry etched on it. Already Mark drew back the bolt, realising that it alone secured the door. A moment later Calamity was in his arms, for once indulging in what she termed "going all woman." With this spasm of reaction over, she raised her face to Mark's and spoke in something like her normal tones.

"What the hell's happening?"

"I'm damned if I know," Mark admitted. "They're mining around here and don't want anybody to learn about it. Now let's get out of here."

"You'll not hear me arguing about that," Calamity assured him fervently.

"Did any of them lay hands on you?"

"The hell they did. I near on split the skull of the only one who tried to come in. Since then nobody's been near except to shove food and water under the door. What is this place, Mark?"

"It'll be one of the cells the fathers used for punishment, or meditation, I reckon."

Swiftly he told her everything he knew, describing the defenses of the place and explaining the plan thought out while coming down the stairs and listening outside the study door. Calamity wondered why he went into so much detail as he himself would be able to tell it to Dusty and the local law when they arrived at Robertstown. Suddenly a chilling thought came to her.

"You're coming with me, aren't you?" she asked.

"If there's a chance, but I don't reckon there will be."

"If you don't come, I'm sticking it out with you."

"No!" Mark growled.

"I'm not running out on you!" the girl stated.

"Don't be *loco*, Calam," Mark said gently. "Most likely we can't both make it out of here. So it's better you go, get word to Dusty and have help in pulling me out."

From what Mark had told her of the guards and other

things, Calamity knew he spoke the truth and made the only possible decision.

"I'll do it, but I'm damned if I like it," she said at last.

"I'm not singing with joy myself," Mark assured her.

"How about when they find I've gone?"

"I'm supposed to have been drugged again, so I'm in the clear."

"Just wait until I get my hands on that skinny——" Calamity spat out, and her views on the Countess could not be printed. "Say, I've an idea."

Collecting a pile of empty sacks, she took them into the cell. At the bed she drew aside the blankets and used the sacks to make a shape which, in the half-light might pass for her lying on it. Drawing the blankets into place, she moved back and surveyed her handiwork.

"It sure looks like you," Mark grinned.

"If we'd more time, I'd give you an answer for that," the girl told him, closing and bolting the door.

Returning to the head of the stairs, Mark blew out the lamp and then inched open the door. Silently, he and Calamity stepped into the passage and moved along it towards the main hall. From the study came sounds of an explosive conversation in Italian, but Mark ignored it. By keeping to the shadows, he and Calamity reached the front wall of the building.

"That's lucky," he told the girl, peering through a window at the wagons. "Nobody's around."

"Why not come with me, we could jump them when they come back."

Much as the idea tempted Mark, cold logic decided him against it. One mistake would bring more help running. Nor would stealing the wagon be any use with the guards at the far end of the gorge. Maybe he and Calamity could sneak by on foot, but their escape would be discovered and armed pursuit on the way long before they reached safety. Nor could Mark chance hiding in the wagon, it might be searched and there was only room for one where he planned for Calamity to hide. So he gave the only possible answer to her suggestion.

"No chance, gal. Play it my way."

"All right," Calamity sighed, and gripped his hand. "I'll be back, Mark."

"I'll be waiting."

"See that you are—and stay clear from the Countess."

With that Calamity moved cautiously to the side of the door, peered out and then darted swiftly through the light into the comforting blackness of the porch. Nobody shouted, warning that she had been seen, so she moved along to the side wall, slipped over the veranda guard and made her way towards the wagons.

Mark waited by the window, trying to see the girl. Lights glowed as the guards returned leading the wagon horses. From the lack of noise Mark guessed that Calamity had not been found, so he turned and made his way to the stairs. Half-way up, he paused and listened. Baton came from somewhere downstairs, followed by three men. Judging by the whip slung over the center man's shoulders, he would be driving the wagon and the other two his escort. Then the study door opened and Mark retreated to the head of the stairs.

"Is everything all right Mr. Baton?" asked the Count.

"Sure," the gun-hand replied.

"Then the Countess and I will go to bed. Good night."

Knowing he could do no more to help Calamity, Mark turned and darted back to his room. On entering, he blew out the small lamp and went to lie on the bed. The precaution paid off. Footsteps approached the door and a light glowed under it, then it opened. The Count

and Countess stood in the doorway and Mark watched
them through his slitted eyelids.

"All seems well," the Count remarked.

"I thought it best to ensure he slept soundly," replied
the Countess.

"So it seems. We had better lock his door, though."

Watching the door close and hearing its lock click,
Mark grinned. If Calamity made good her escape—and
the lack of noise led him to believe she had—there
would be nothing to connect him with it.

A problem faced Calamity as she reached the wagons.
Which one would be used by the men? Given a choice
she would take the one furthest from the house and so
gambled on her judgment. The gamble paid off. Even as
she ducked beneath the wagon, Calamity saw the men
approaching. At first she could not see the purpose of
bringing six horses, then remembered there would be
two guards along. Instead of riding in the wagon, they
must be using the horses. Perhaps Mark could have hid
away after all. Calamity realised it was too late to worry
about that.

Reaching up, Calamity felt at the bottom of the
wagon. The possum-belly was in place; a rawhide sheet
nailed underneath and used as a repository for wood
during long hauls over country which did not offer a
supply of fuel for fires. While it would not be used on
the shorter trip to Robertstown, traveling to the other
side of the Wapiti hills called for its services.

Fortunately the possum-belly held nothing and Calamity drew herself up into it. By curling up, she could
lay fairly comfortably and hoped to make the entire
journey under the wagon. Although unable to see anything, her ears told her all she needed to know. The
hitching of the team went by without incident, but feet
thudded on the wagon bed above her as boxes for the
supplies were loaded. Calamity knew that Mark called

the play right. Had he been in the back, the men would have found him.

At last all appeared to be ready. The wagon rocked as its driver swung on to the box. Leather creaked and horses moved restlessly while being mounted. Some comments Calamity could not understand passed, a whip cracked and she felt a jolt as the wagon started to move.

Curled up in the possum-belly, Calamity found less discomfort than she expected. Much in the way that a hammock yielded to the motion of a ship, the sheet of rawhide absorbed the swaying and jolting of the wagon. Calamity's life made her used to accepting hardships and she found the possum-belly no worse a bed than circumstances more than once forced her to use. Having slept little since recovering in the cell, exhaustion began to draw her eyelids together. At first she tried to fight it off, then began to doze. Bumps caused by the uneven trail surface jolted her awake, but each time she dropped into a doze again.

Waking on the lurch of the wagon passing over a lump in the trail, Calamity found it to be daylight. Not merely dawn, but some time after or she missed her guess. Carefully she peeked out of the possum-belly's side. The escort rode up front, most likely talking with the driver. Instead of being in a gorge, the trail ran along either the top or side of a valley. Down below Calamity could see a river; the Wapiti most likely. Beyond it, open range instead of those brooding slopes and walls.

Suddenly Calamity became aware of light behind her. Turning, she realised that the rawhide did not hold her as snugly as when she first climbed in. Even before seeing the gap at the rear end of the possum-belly she guessed what had happened. Weakened by long use und lack of care, the rawhide had torn free, ripping away at the nail heads that should hold it in place. While Calamity watched, another nail parted company with the hide.

Never had Calamity's courage been put to such a test. All too well she knew the fate awaiting her if the men found her, but did not allow the thought to make her panic.

Swiftly judging the wagon's speed, she decided it to be no more than a walk. Wriggling around, she forced apart the widening slit until it joined the opening at the side. Free from restraint, she slid down on the trail, lying so that the wheels missed her and turning on to her back. As the wagon passed over her she rose and gripped its tailboard. With a lithe swing, she drew herself up and aboard.

Absorbed in conversation with his companions, the driver did not suspect Calamity's presence in the wagon. Creeping forward silently, she saw the handle of a whip hanging over the back of the driver's seat. Not just an ordinary whip, but her own. It seemed like an omen. Bounding to the front of the wagon, Calamity landed on the seat by the driver. She snatched the reins from his hands, giving out a screech loud enough to scare the hair from a wooden cigar-store Indian. Before the driver recovered from his shock, Calamity drove her elbow savagely into his ribs. Startled by the yell, the horses lunged forward and hit their harness with enough force to jerk the wagon violently. The combination of the jerk and Calamity's attack pitched the driver from his seat, tumbling him almost on to the guard riding at the right side.

Twisting around, Calamity peered back through the canopy of the wagon and found that she had had a stroke of luck. When the driver almost fell on it, the guard's horse shied away and reared on its hind legs. Taken by surprise its rider slipped backwards over its rump and landed on the trail. Any jubilation she might

have felt was tempered by the knowledge that a second
guard accompanied the wagon.

Calamity did not need to think about where the second man might be. Already his horse appeared alongside the wagon. Unlike the Countess' escort of the previous day, the man carried a revolver at his belt. Drawing
it, he yelled something which Calamity took to be a
command for her to halt.

"Like hell!" she gritted, releasing the reins with one
hand so as to scoop up her whip.

Lining his gun, the man fired. Although at close
range, shooting at a moving target from the back of a
fast-running horse called for more skill than the man
possessed and his bullet missed Calamity. Nor did he
come too close to the wagon. Although she thought the
range might be too great, Calamity cut loose with her
whip. It missed the man, but struck the horse on the
neck. Letting out a squeal of pain, the horse arched its
back in a buck which almost unseated its rider. Almost
but not quite. While he lost his revolver, the man stayed
afork the horse and let Calamity forge ahead while he
brought it under control.

Despite the respite, Calamity knew herself to be far
from out of danger. The horses pulling the wagon met
with her approval, being bred for the work. Yet no
amount of breeding could give the strength to out-run
saddle mounts when hauling a wagon.

Striking a hole in the trail, the wagon lurched violently. Calamity felt the jolt and the reins ripped from
her left hand. Grabbing desperately, she clung to the
seat and avoided being thrown off. One glance told her
that she might have been better off if she had been
pitched out. The two horses stretched out at full speed;
not a bad thing, one might assume, except for a small,
vital detail. Let a horse start galloping when spooked
and its age-old instinct for flight took hold. Without
control the two horses hauling the wagon would build

up speed, but in a blind panic. Already they had reached the point where control would be difficult even if she held the ribbons. But she did not, they trailed wildly along out of her reach.

Training caused Calamity to act. She threw a glance behind as the wagon rocked, bounced and pitched over the trail. Already the second guard regained control of his horse and halted its pain-inspired bucking. Beyond him, the second man had caught his horse and mounted, ignoring the shouting, gesticulating driver. It seemed that the second guard wanted support before coming up against Calamity again, for he twisted in his saddle, waved and shouted to his mounted companion.

Calamity forgot the men after that quick glance. Grabbing the brake handle, she heaved back on it and felt the shoes clamp home on the wheels. Then the wagon gave a wrenching lurch and something metallic cracked under the box. It was a sound Calamity recognized and one which filled her with mingled emotions. The connecting pin had broken, freeing the doubletree from the wagon. Already the horses drew ahead as the brakes slowed the wagon.

Ahead the trail curved around a corner and the valley fell away in a sheer drop to the river some fifty feet below. On a down-grade, travelling at speed the horses could never have made the turn hampered by the wagon. Without it, they swung around. Not so the wagon. Sliding forward under its own momentum, it went off the trail and plunged downwards.

CHAPTER TWELVE

It Can All Belong To Us, Mark

"Ooh! My head!" moaned Sheila, sitting on the edge of the bed.

At the sound of her voice, Mark turned and looked in her direction from where he stood by the window. Whatever kind of drug the Countess used, it worked well. Since succumbing to it in the small hours of the morning, Sheila had not woke; in fact she hardly moved. Thinking back on how he felt on waking from a dose of the drug, Mark concluded that the wine drunk by Sheila must not mix with the sleeping draught. Certainly he did not feel as ill as the girl looked.

Despite his concern for Calamity's welfare, Mark managed to sleep after being locked into his room. On waking, he rose and went to the window. From the position of the sun, he concluded the time to be around nine o'clock. Apart from a throbbing ache from the worst bruising, he felt no ill-effects from his fight with *Il Bruto*. A wash, shave and change of shirt would set him up on his feet and prepare him for whatever the day held. One thing was for sure. Sheila did not look in any shape to require his attentions.

Suddenly the girl clutched at her stomac'., rose and made a hurried dash to the door. Mark wo.dered what she would make of finding it locked, but the situation did not arise. Apparently somebody had come along and unlocked it, for Sheila jerked it open and he heard her feet clatter away down the passage.

The servant who handed out the drugged drinks made his appearance, carrying a bowl of steaming water. After Mark satisfied his toilet requirements, the man gave what appeared to be a request to follow him. Instead of making for the big diningroom, Mark found himself led downstairs.

"Good morning, Mr. Counter," greeted the Count, rising from the table as Mark entered the room next to his study. "I trust you slept well?"

"Well enough," Mark replied.

"You must join us for breakfast," the Countess told him, and he saw just a hint of triumph in her eyes.

Although the Count wore a robe and gave the appearance of being fresh out of bed, his wife had her usual clothes on, including the riding boots, and the quirt hung from the back of the chair. Mark decided that she might not be entirely unaware of Sheila's feelings and did not intend to give the other a chance to catch her defenseless.

Taking the offered seat, Mark studied his host and hostess. He could see nothing in their attitude to tell him that they knew of Calamity's escape. The absence of Baton tended to make Mark believe that nothing was suspected.

"Calam should have made Robertstown by now," he said, watching the Count carefully.

Nothing showed on the Count's face to make Mark think that Calamity's escape had been discovered. In fact the blond giant realized that he had made the kind of comment his host and hostess expected.

"She will have," the Count agreed smoothly. "Of course it will be late afternoon before she arrives. Until

then we must find something to entertain you. I believe
Sheila is indisposed.''

"She looked that way," Mark replied. "How're you
figuring on explaining what happened to *Il Bruto* to the
law?"

"As an accident, if you will co-operate," replied the
Count.

"Perhaps if Mr. Counter saw our little secret he might
be more understanding, Alberto," the Countess put in.

Only for a moment did doubt waver on the Count's
face, then he nodded. "Of course he may. Will you
show him, my dear, while I write out a report for him to
deliver to the sheriff's office at Robertstown."

"We'll go as soon as breakfast is over," the Countess
replied. "I'm sure you will find it interesting, Mr.
Counter."

During breakfast, both the Count and Countess did
their best to put Mark at ease. He realised that nothing
could make *Il Bruto's* death pass as an accident without
his cooperation. However the stress put on his evidence
to the sheriff was more to keep him believing that he
would be allowed to leave when the doctor arrived, of
that Mark felt certain.

With breakfast over, the Countess escorted Mark to a
door which had been locked on the previous day. Instead of leading to a ruined section of the mission it
opened up into a cellar. Leading the way, the Countess
took Mark down a flight of stairs and into a tunnel
which stretched off into the distance. Mark had once
been into the shaft of a mine and found himself in the
same surroundings; or almost the same. Instead of
timbers, the walls appeared to be shored up with pieces
from wagons.

"This doesn't look too safe," he said.

"Oh, it's safe enough," the Countess replied. "Do
you think the men you saw last night would continue to

work down here if it wasn't?''

Mark did not reply, but looked around him with interest. Far ahead he could hear the sound of digging and voices.

"What are you after?" he asked.

"Gold," breathed the Countess. "A vein of gold that will make your California mines look like chicken-feed. Do you want to go further in?"

"I'm a cowhand, not a miner. So I'd rather have the sky over head."

"Come then, we will go upstairs and let you see it."

For all her assurance about the tunnel's safety, the Countess barely hid her relief when she returned to the ground floor. She returned with Mark to the main hall, after showing him where the miners and guards slept, and suggested that they took a stroll in the fresh air.

Leaving the house, they walked together around to the rear and stood looking along the valley. Far down it Mark could see his horse but knew there was no chance of getting to it. He sensed that the Countess brought him outside for more than a breath of fresh air, and thought back to how she acted while they were alone in the diningroom the previous afternoon.

"Are you interested in what I just showed you?" she asked, after talking about inconsequential matters for a time.

"Everybody's interested in gold," Mark replied. "Trouble being finding it."

"It's there all right!" she told him eagerly.

Mark sensed that the Countess meant to come to the point real soon and guessed at the best way to keep her talking.

"So's Jim Bowie's Lost Mine," he told her. "You can buy 'secret' maps telling where to find it."

One glance told him that he had struck the right line.

"I assure you that we are not relying on some fake

'secret' map!'' she snapped. ''The gold is there.''

''You sound real sure.''

''I *am* real sure. I won't go into the full story of how, but my husband came into possession of a report written by the senior priest of this mission. Like most of its kind, the mission here combined work with religion. They chose this site to search for iron—and found gold.''

''Then why didn't they exploit it?'' asked Mark. ''From what I've heard, the mission didn't object to running at a profit.''

''At the time of the discovery, the Mexican Government was in the process of handing this territory over to the United States. Being a patriot, the priest decided to prevent your people from benefiting by the discovery. He closed the mission and started out for Old Mexico. On the way, his entire party was wiped out by hostile Indians.''

''Then how did you learn about it?''

''The priest made out a full report of his find and hid it in a compartment built secretly in a deed box. A party of U.S. Cavalry found the box and a few other items left by the raiders at the scene of the massacre and returned it to the bishop of the mission's order. Eventually my husband came into possession of the box and stumbled on its secret by accident, the bishop had not known about the hidden compartment it seems. Alberto is much cleverer than he looks, Mark. He read the report and saw its possibilities straight away. We were visiting in the East at the time and it proved easy to arrange for a 'hunting' trip out here. One visit to the mission convinced Alberto of the document's authenticity. Before leaving, the priests collapsed all the shafts they had dug, but Albert knew they could be reopened.''

While speaking, the Countess continued to walk and led Mark into a hollow from which they would be out of sight of the mission. Sitting on the grass, she indicated that he join her.

"So all you had to do was get the gold out," Mark said, settling down at her side.

"Yes. Alberto did not want anybody to know of the mine. You know what would have happened if word leaked out."

"Sure," agreed Mark. "I've seen a gold-rush start and what came after it."

"Our work would be made much more difficult had it become known, so we returned to New York and made plans."

"Then those Italian jaspers aren't after his scalp?"

"The Mafia?" laughed the Countess. "Alberto is one of their leaders. They supplied us with our bodyguards, located Baton and Whales and gave us the excuse to cut ourselves off from society. Everybody believed that Alberto had been threatened, sympathized with him and gave him assistance. When we came West, we brought letters from high sources which kept the local law from bothering us. Whales picked the men, selecting those without dependants who might wish to accompany them or who they would want to visit. Baton brought the men and supplies here secretly. To prevent anybody suspecting how many people lived here, we alternated between three towns, buying supplies in each. None of them realised that what we bought did not last us the full period between visits. Fresh meat was a problem, but Baton solved it by taking men out and butchering beef on the range. Slow-elking I think you call it."

"That's what we call it," Mark agreed. "You were lucky you didn't get caught at it."

"He only went out when rain seemed imminent, so it washed out tracks and traces of the butchering."

"And nobody found out?"

"Baton had to silence a man on three occasions,

bringing his horse and body back to the valley."

With an effort Mark prevented his true feelings from showing at the callous words. He had never known such a woman as the Countess, but began to understand a few things about her.

"Have you found the gold?" he asked, not daring to chance his emotions if she told him any more about the murder of the three cowhands.

"Enough to feel sure we are on the right track. The work is not easy using the primitive methods forced on to us. We daren't chance bringing in modern equipment until we're sure it will pay us. Nor can we get timber to shore up the tunnels without drawing attention to ourselves."

"Don't the men object to working under those conditions?"

"We make their lives so comfortable that they accept the risks."

"With whing-dings like last night?" Mark suggested.

"We don't go so far every day," the Countess admitted. "Alberto used similar tactics to those of the ancient Romans when the population grew restless."

"Was that why he brought in the lions?"

"One reason. Another is that they prevent attempts at desertion far more than the presence of the armed guards. The lions added spice to the entertainment. At first we could drive a horse or bull in for them to kill——"

"And wound up tossing human beings in," Mark said bitterly.

"I wanted no part of it, Mark," the Countess assured him, so sincerely he almost believed her. "It began by accident. There was a fight at a dinner and *Il Bruto* knocked his opponent over the veranda by accident. Instead of being horrified, the crowd revelled in the sight. From then on, each time we had a trouble-causer among the men, *Il Bruto* was told to pick a fight and the loser went to the lions.'' She gripped Mark's hands tight in her own, looking pleadingly at him. ''I had no idea that he would pick on you, Mark. But you defeated him and all is well.''

''How do you mean?'' Mark inquired, sensing that she would soon come to the point of why she brought him to the hollow.

''There's a fortune to be made here,'' the Countess answered.

''So?''

''It can all belong to us, Mark.''

For a moment Mark did not reply, but he understood almost everything on hearing the words.

''Us?'' he finally said.

''We can take over the entire thing,'' the Countess replied.

''Against your husband and all his men?''

''Why not?'' asked the Countess, moving closer. ''Already the guards have heard of your strength and skill with a gun. I can control them if they know you are with me.''

''How about Baton, Whales and the miners?''

''Whaley will work for whoever pays him. By beating *Il Bruto* you won over the miners.''

''And Baton?''

''He will have to die. I tr—I know he is too loyal to Alberto to change sides.''

''And how do I take him, without a gun?'' asked Mark. ''He's a gun fighter, and a good one.''

''I can get your gunbelt and Colts, then you can meet him on even terms. There's a great future for us here, Mark. We can continue as Alberto does. Do you know that he has not paid the men any wages yet? They need none, we feed them, clothe them and supply them with entertainment. When they get the gold——''

"Is that why you brought me here?" Mark asked as the Countess let her words tail off.

"Yes. From the first moment I saw you, I knew——"

Suspicion flickered on her face and again she stopped speaking without completing her sentence. Mark scooped her into his arms and kissed her, throwing all he had into it. On releasing her, he smiled down into her face.

"It's sure lucky that I collapsed on the trail then."

"It was the most fortunate thing that ever happened to either of us," the Countess answered, breathing hard.

"Why do you reckon you can trust me?" asked Mark.

"You like money, that's obvious. A working cow-hand does not dress as well as you unless he is—shall we say open to ways of augmenting his salary."

The words explained one of the last things puzzling Mark. Few people outside his immediate circle of friends knew of his financial standing and the Countess drew the wrong conclusion. Wrong or not, it gave Mark a chance to regain possession of his guns. It also made his position a damned sight more dangerous. Let the Countess just once doubt him and she would not hesitate to order his death. In making him such an offer, she placed her own life in his hands. From what Mark had seen, the Count would never forgive her for plotting against him and had shown that he placed no value on human life.

"When do we start?" Mark inquired.

"As soon as I can get your guns, but I doubt if there will be a chance before tomorrow morning."

"Calam'll have the doctor here before then," Mark pointed out.

Only for a moment did the Countess hesitate. Once more she proved herself capable of real fast thought.

Nothing on her face showed that she believed Calamity was still a prisoner and could not send the doctor from Robertstown.

"You can tell him that you still don't feel up to travelling," she said.

"Reckon your husband'll think anything about it?"

"We can say you're interested in working for him. Now we had better get back to the house before he becomes suspicious."

As the Countess and Mark walked towards the door of her husband's study, a man burst out of the cellar where Calamity had been held prisoner. Dashing up to the Countess, he broke into a spate of Italian, accompanied by arm waving and pointing. Even without knowing the language, Mark could guess that Calamity's disappearance had at last been noticed.

"What!" spat the Countess in English, and swung towards Mark. Suspicion and fury showed on her face, to be replaced by bewilderment. With an almost visible effort, she regained control of herself. "A domestic upset, Mark," she said. "I must tell my husband."

Mark could almost follow her line of thought. On hearing of Calamity's escape, the Countess first thought that Mark was involved. Then she remembered that she sent him a drugged drink and saw him locked in his room.

In the study, the Count almost mirrored his wife's reactions as she told him and Baton the news. Questions spat back and forwards in Italian. Glances were flung at Mark who maintained a look of innocent interest as if waiting to learn what caused all the fuss. Clearly the Count refused to accept that Mark might have tricked him in some way, and the Countess went along with his refusal.

"Organize a search, Katherine," the Count ordered in Italian. "You keep him out of the way, Baton."

"Look, Counter," Baton said, turning to Mark.

"The Count's got some trouble. What say we go look in on the girls?"

"I never refused *that* yet." Mark replied with a grin. "Unless I can lend a hand——"

"No, I can manage, Mr. Counter," the Count told him. "It would bore you and I would not wish a guest to be bored."

A combined bar and diningroom had been fitted up for the workers in the rear of the building. Although all the men were at work, several of the girls sat around and gathered in a group when Mark entered with Baton. After telling Mark that Sheila had retired to bed, the girls began to talk and make themselves pleasant. Cards were produced and a merry game of poker commenced.

Almost an hour passed and the Countess entered the room. Ignoring the girls, she came over and whispered to Baton. Mark could see that she brought interesting and important news, but failed to guess what it might be.

"That trouble out front's over now," Baton told Mark, returning to the table.

"Pleased to hear it," Mark answered, sounding polite but disinterested.

"I've got to go back to work," the gun-hand went on. "Want to come?"

"Not me, I'm a dollar fifty down and hate to quit a loser."

For all his levity, Mark felt worried. Maybe Calamity had been discovered under the wagon. Yet it did not seem likely that the men could have returned so soon with the wagon and their retrieved prisoner. He knew he could do nothing and must continue to play the game to the bitter end. Fortunately none of the girls had the intelligence to notice the change in his attitude, for Mark felt a weight of worry growing heavier on him.

"She escaped in the wagon, Baton," the Countess said as they returned to the study. "And died in it when it went over a cliff. Luigi and the other two just returned with the news.''

"I want to know how she escaped," Baton growled.

"She could have worked open the bolt from inside and the door upstairs wasn't locked," answered the Countess. "Then she hid in the wagon. That was a shrewd woman."

"Too shrewd," the Count put in.

"Why don't we keep a tighter hold on Counter?" demanded Baton, expressing a thought which had occurred to Mark.

"You've not seen how strong he is," the Countess replied. "Try to lock him up and you'll have nothing but trouble. So far he doesn't suspect anything, so we can leave him free and avoid it."

"Who do you reckon he's working for?" asked Baton. "If he's wanting to spy on us, he's not doing it for fun."

The Countess had already thought out an answer to that question. "Perhaps he was hired by the Mafia to check up on our progress, Alberto."

"Who, Mark Counter?" snorted Baton.

"We don't know for sure he is Mark Counter," the Countess pointed out. "You have never met him before, Mr. Baton."

"He fits most of what I've heard about Counter."

"I never before saw a working cowhand who dressed so well," the Countess stated.

"There's that to it," Baton agreed. "Counter allows to be a dandy, though."

"Then he would be an ideal choice for our man to pretend to be," the Countess said.

"He's not Italian," Baton remarked.

"Neither are you, or Mr. Whales, but the Mafia reached and hired you," the Countess answered. "He knows nothing of the girl being here, her escape or death. I say we continue acting towards Mr. Counter, or whoever he is, as we have from the start. If he should be working for the Mafia, we must not harm him.''

''That's true,'' breathed the Count, knowing all too well the way of the Mafia with anybody who crossed it. ''That would be their way, sending a non-Italian, if they wished to learn how my scheme is going.''

''Then we must not harm him,'' insisted the Countess. ''Let him see what he will and leave when he is ready, Alberto.''

''And when he doesn't hear from the girl?'' asked Baton.

''We will face *that* when it comes,'' replied the Countess.

Not knowing that the Countess had given him a reason for being at the Mission, Mark spent a quiet day. At times he felt a change in the atmosphere, but could not place it. Certainly he saw nothing to make him suspect that Calamity's escape bid failed. The second wagon had gone from its place when Mark finally left his card game with the girls, but he accepted Baton's explanation that it went to gather firewood or other fuel from beyond the hills.

Sheila did not make an appearance, but the Countess told Mark that the blonde had work to do. Only on special occasions were the miners and girls allowed into the well-furnished quarters of their employers, and Sheila, as boss of the female staff, ran the bar where the men spent their leisure hours.

Towards evening Mark acted as he would be expected to, by asking about Calamity's non-arrival with the doctor. He appeared to accept the Count's suggestion that maybe the doctor had other work and agreed to stay on another day. In doing so, Mark temporarily quietened the Count's suspicions.

By evening he had formed a fair idea of how the Mission ran. While not condoning any part of the operation, he had to admit that the Count showed considerable ingenuity in bringing it about. Of course only a small part of the building had luxurious furnishings and glass windows, but the miners lived in no worse conditions than they would in any other employment; and the entertainment supplied kept them content. It had been quite a task, shipping in everything needed without the surrounding districts hearing, but the Count's men accomplished it and Mark could admire the skill and organising ability which brought it about.

Nobody troubled to lock his door that night and, just as he was dropping off to sleep, he heard it open. A moment later he felt a warm shape wriggle into bed alongside him. Two slim arms locked about his neck and a mouth pressed passionately against his.

"It's safe, Alberto's asleep," purred the Countess' voice. "Tomorrow is his day to inspect the mine workings. I will be able to get you your gunbelt while he does it."

"Good," Mark replied.

"If we work this properly, Mark," the Countess went on, clinging to him and nuzzling at his cheek eagerly. "By tomorrow night we will own all this."

"Likely," said Mark.

"You'll have to pay me for making you rich," she went on. "And you can start right now."

While talking in whispers, they made sufficient noise to prevent them hearing certain sounds from the passage which might otherwise have given them a grim warning of danger.

CHAPTER THIRTEEN

I've Been Waiting For This

Judging by the way she acted, the Countess was not indulging in her first clandestine love affair. About an hour before dawn broke she swung herself from the bed, planted a kiss on Mark's face and whispered that she would see him at breakfast. Then she glided from his room. When her husband woke he would find her where a loving and dutiful wife should be, at his side.

Mark dozed off after she left. Making advance payment for a chance to escape had been exhausting, the way the Countess wanted it. Daylight woke him and he rose, drew on his levis and looked around the room.

"Mark!" screamed the Countess, voice. "Help!"

Springing across the room, Mark threw open the door and lunged out. He saw the men flanking the door just an instant too late. Something hard and round thrust between his legs to catch against his shins and trip him. Although he managed to throw up his arms and shield his head from direct contact with the opposite wall, he still rammed it with sufficient force to drop him in a dazed heap to the floor. Men sprang on him, hands dragging his arms behind his back, ropes encircling and pinning his wrists. By the time Mark recovered from the collision, he found himself to be securely hog-tied.

"You sure saved us some trouble, friend," Baton said, standing with three of the Italian guards and looking down at Mark. In his hands he held a shotgun, the barrels of which had been used to trip Mark. "I thought we'd have to come in after you."

"So you got me," Mark answered. "What now?"

"That's up to the Count," Baton drawled. "You've riled him, friend, you and his wife. I don't envy either of you."

Sitting up in bed, the Countess looked around her. First she found that her husband had already rose and left the room, she wriggled her toes as an excited sensation ran through her. This was the day for which she waited ever since arriving at the Mission and learning of its potentiality for wealth. And what a partner the fates brought to help her achieve her desires. Never had she met such a man as Mark Counter, one so completely capable of satisfying her passion and so well equipped to make her plans work. It was fortunate that Baton refused her first tentative advances and so did not receive the offer she made Mark.

At which point the Countess realised that her quirt did not lie in its usual place on the bed-side chair. Nor could she see her riding boots in the room.

Rising from the bed, she walked to the door and opened it, meaning to call for the servant and ask where he put her property. Before she could speak, the sound of voices and a feminine giggle reached her ears. Wondering which of the girls had the audacity to be in the main diningroom at that hour, the Countess collected her robe, drew it on and went to investigate.

Perhaps at another time the sight of her husband seated on the divan with Sheila close to him would have rung a warning bell for the Countess, but at that moment, she had a head full of her own plans. So she advanced into the big room, clean forgetting that she omitted to take a basic precaution.

"What's this, Alberto?" she hissed.

"Sheila has brought a puzzle to me, my dear," the Count replied, making no attempt to move away from the girl. "Apparently I sent word to her that she must remain with the other girls as two planned to persuade some of the men to steal an amount of our gold and escape from the valley. She claims you told her, my dear. Most commendable—only I did not say any such thing."

"So?" the Countess replied. "I knew this—she—wouldn't obey unless I said the order came from you."

"But why give it?"

"I heard there might be trouble and took steps to prevent it. I have before without complaint."

"And there was no other reason?" asked the Count.

"What other reason could there be?" his wife snapped back.

"Perhaps a wish to keep Sheila away from Mr. Counter."

"And why would I do that?"

"So that you could go sleep with him," Sheila put in.

"How dare you?" the Countess yelled and suddenly realised she did not wear her riding boots or carry the quirt which had been the dominant factors in her control over the hired woman.

"Don't waste time, dearie," Sheila purred. "I talked to the girls, none of them knew anything about it. So I came up this end and waited around. Sure enough, after a while you came sneaking out of your room and straight down to Mark. So I woke Albie here and we sneaked down. You didn't talk loud, but we heard enough."

"Alberto!" gasped the Countess, desperately trying a bluff. "Are you——."

"It's between Sheila and yourself, my dear," answered the Count.

Slowly Sheila rose to her feet, her magnificent body

quivering under the saloongirl's dress. "I've been waiting for this," she said.

Suddenly the Countess knew why she could not find her boots or quirt. Fear knifed into her and she turned to dash for the door.

"Mark!" she screamed as she reached the passage and her voice echoed along it. "Help!"

Fingers dug into the Countess' hair from behind and she felt herself being dragged backwards into the diningroom. Hissing in satisfaction, Sheila swung the Countess around and sent her hurling bodily across the room. All the bottled-up hatred came boiling out as Sheila saw the Countess reeling away. Eagerly the voluptuous blonde charged forward to make the most of the chance Alberto gave her when he hid his wife's boots and quirt.

The Count half-rose from his seat as he saw the raw fury which replaced fear on his wife's face. Managing to catch her balance, the Countess did not fall, her fingers lashed out at hair as Sheila hurtled towards her. Although Sheila's weight and impetus brought them both down, the Countess gave a heave which rolled the heavier blonde over and landed on top of her. Fingers tore at hair, raked nails across flesh and screams of rage broke from two mouths as the women rolled over and over.

For the first time in his life the Count saw two women fight. While watching, he felt his throat grow dry and a surge of emotion that he had never known before. There was something wildly exciting about the raw, primeval rage exhibited as the women churned over and over which made *Il Bruto's* efforts appear mild and exceeded even the sight of a human being torn apart by lions. The Count wondered why he had not thought of such a diversion for his dinners. Maybe the time would come when he needed something extra to make his employees forget the dangers of their working conditions and such a fight ought to do the trick especially with a promise of more of the same.

During the period she had known her present employers, Sheila often thought of what she aimed to do to the Countess when the opportunity arose. With her background and upbringing she expected no trouble in handling the other woman, assuming that when the time came everything would go her way. The time had come, she found herself tangled with the woman she had hated for so long—only things did not go all her way. In fact the Countess proved to be more of a handful, not the terrified weakling Sheila expected. One of the things Sheila overlooked was that the Countess' way of life kept her far fitter than did Sheila's, another being that the backgrounds of herself and the Countess had once been pretty much the same. All Sheila knew was that the Countess showed considerable ability in fighting back against her attack.

Not that any thought, skill or planned effort showed in the fight, only animal rage, blind and merciless as nails, teeth, elbows, knees and almost every other part of the body gave or took punishment. The Countess lost her robe, half wriggling from it and half having it dragged off her back in the churning melee. In losing it, she rolled away from Sheila and lurched to her feet. No longer did she look cool, aloof and attractive. Fingernails had left bloody furrows down her left cheek, blood dribbled from the corner of her mouth and the bestial rage she felt swept all traces of charm from her features.

Not that Sheila looked much better. Her blonde hair now had the appearance of a dirty wet woolen mop and a blow from the Countess' bony fists caused a swollen discoloration to her right eye. Forcing herself into a kneeling position, she sucked down a gulp of air, and flung herself at the Countess.

Instead of waiting for the attack, the Countess charged to meet it. The two women came together, teeth and nails seeking flesh, screaming what they may have thought to be curses but which came out as no more than mindless sounds of rage and pain.

While trying to close in, Sheila felt the Countess' fingers dig into her bust. Pain ripped into the blonde and she jerked back to throw a roundhouse punch which smashed into the center of the Countess' face. Squealing in agony, her nose spurting blood, the Countess lost her hold. Quick to follow up her advantage, although instinctive rather than conscious thought drove her, Sheila moved in and rammed her knee into the Countess's groin. Sheila had done the same thing in bar-room brawls and always the recipient doubled over, screaming or gasping in agony, then collapsed. Although the Countess screamed and doubled over, she kept on her feet and locked her arms around the other woman in a desperate effort to prevent herself going down. Sheila tore at her hair, rained blows to her head and tried to kick; which did not prove successful due to her losing her shoes in the first wild tangle on the floor.

Sick with pain, the Countess clawed weakly upwards, her fingers closing on the neck of Sheila's dress and ripping at it. Then her nails tore raw gashes across the blonde's ample chest. Again and again the Countess tore at Sheila, keeping her own head down. In desperation Sheila tried to twist away, swinging around so as to get behind the Countess. Suddenly the Countess straightened up, driving the top of her head with sickening force under Sheila's jaw. Back reeled Sheila, her eyes glassy and head spinning. The impact also dazed the Countess, causing her to stagger and almost fall. Recovering her balance, she flung herself at Sheila and, hitting the blonde, forced her backwards through the window on to the balcony.

Carrying Sheila before her, the Countess forced the blonde back against the balcony wall and bent her over it to rain blows on her face and upper body. His face showing lust and excitement, the Count halted at the windows, wondering if his wife knew where she was and what to do. Probably the Countess did not at first. Sheila's hands were on her face, shoving back at it while her legs tried to entwine around the slim body. By accident the Countess hooked an arm under Sheila's right leg and heaved, raising the blonde and dumping her on top of the wall.

Realization came to both women at the same moment. Sheila screamed in terror as her legs tipped over the wall. Desperately she threw her arms around the Countess' neck, clinging on with all her strength. At the same time, the Countess thrust at Sheila's body, forcing it over the edge of the wall. Once Sheila managed to hook a leg back, but the Countess shoved it off again. Although she had Sheila hanging over the ledge, the Countess could not free herself from the blonde's clinging arms. The weight dragged the Countess further and further forward and her hands clawed at Sheila's shoulders in an attempt to break the hold.

Attracted by the noise, the lions gathered below. They had been fed from the balcony often enough to associate it with food and prowled underneath, eyes studying the dangling woman.

Staring at his wife's half-naked body, the Count licked his lips nervously. Although he knew her to be ruthless and evil-tempered, he never suspected her to be capable of such fury. Should she survive the fight, his life would be in constant jeopardy. Even without that, Katherine deserved to die for her treachery.

He stepped forward, bending to grip the Countess around the legs. Before she realised her danger, he straightened and swung her feet from the floor. The weight of Sheila on the Countess' neck did the rest. Twin screams of terror rang briefly as they fell, still locked in each other's grasp. Even before the women landed, the lion sprang and all three went crashing down. Leaping in from the left, one of the lionesses crushed the Countess' skull with a paw-blow and the lion's teeth closed on the top of Sheila's head.

On the balcony, the Count glared down. He watched his wife die without a single qualm. After he took her from a humble position as governess to a wealthy British family, married her, gave her his name, she plotted against him. That after he gave her his name; a name of one of Italy's oldest families; which, unless he missed his guess, went back to the Caesars. Katherine betrayed that name. It was only fitting that a descendant of the Caesars used one of their methods to dispose of enemies.

Well, Katherine was dead and he did not need to fear her scheming. When his men struck the main vein of ore, he could carry on with his plans. With that amount of wealth he could build a home worthy of Caesar. Instead of a paltry three lions, he would be able to afford all the trappings of the circus, chariot-racing, gladiators, everything.

With a shudder the Count forced himself back to reality. When the lions finished feeding, he would order the enclosure cleaned out. That meant driving the animals into the lean-to and locking its door; a ticklish business. The last time they tried it, one of the lionesses made good her escape. Unfortunately she escaped from the valley, or he could have enjoyed hunting her down.

Without another glance at the enclosure, the Count walked back into the dining room and crossed to its door. He found Baton approaching along the passage and asked, "Did you get Counter?"

"Yep. I stayed on to make sure they tied him good. It sounded like quite a fight in here."

"It was," enthused the Count. "I'm sorry you missed it, but perhaps later we can arrange another."

"Thanks," Baton said dryly. "Who won?"

"I'm afraid they both fell into the enclosure," replied the Count calmly.

Baton looked at his boss for a long moment and made a wry face. "How about Counter?"

"Let us go and see him," the Count beamed. "What I have in mind may make up for your disappointment at missing the fight."

Walking along the passage, the two men came to where Mark lay bound hand and foot on the floor.

"Well, Mr. Counter," the Count said. "What are we going to do with you?"

"Feed me to your lions, likely," Mark answered.

"I thought of that," admitted the Count. "Unfortunately they have received too much food already."

"I'm in no hurry," Mark drawled.

"A sense of humor," the Count whooped. "And courage, Mr. Baton. What a pity. What a pity. You are Mark Counter, aren't you?"

"I've never denied it," Mark drawled.

"What would you have done if Katherine gave you your guns?"

"Used them to get out of here."

"You know, Mr. Counter, I believe you," the Count said. "Which makes it unfortunate. If you left, the law would hear of my little entertainments and I doubt if they would approve. So you're going to die."

"How?" asked Baton.

"Katherine told me that Mr. Counter was a strong man. As strong as a horse were her exact words. And seeing how he handled *Il Bruto*, I believe her."

"So?" Mark wanted to know.

"So I wonder if you are as strong as *two* horses. To find out, I mean to have you taken outside, fastened between two horses and see if you are strong enough to save yourself from being torn apart."

CHAPTER FOURTEEN

They've Got Mark, Dusty.

As the wagon tipped forward over the edge of the trail, Calamity figured she had a mighty short life expectancy. She also decided that she would try to prolong it as much as possible. While reaching both conclusions, her instincts caused the remainder of her to act. Rising, she dived over the side and away from the falling wagon. Several boxes and barrels tumbled out of the front, but Calamity had thrown herself clear and they missed her. Instinct caused her to raise her arms, the right hand still gripping the whip, over her head as she had done more than once when diving into a river for a pleasure swim. Down she plunged, striking the water with a breathtaking impact. An instant later the wagon's contents arrived, then the wagon itself. Under the surface of the river, Calamity felt an unseen force suddenly jerk at her and thrust her savagely towards the opposite bank.

For what seemed like an endless time Calamity was pushed along, unable to surface. Then her head broke water, to touch stone. A momentary panic hit her and she fought it down to reason out where she might be. Glancing around gave her the answer. At that point the river had scooped out a cave under the river bank, a deep, still pool beneath the rock but not quite touching

it at the present water level. While it might be an interesting rock formation, Calamity wanted only to leave
and carry out her mission.

"Hold it, hot-head!" she told herself. "You had
company, remember."

At which she became aware of the whip still clutched
firmly in her grasp. Lowering her legs, she found her
feet just touched the bottom while her head poked
above the surface. Hanging the whip around her neck,
she looked across the river. By inching forward cautiously, Calamity moved into a position where she could
see the top of the cliff over which the wagon plunged.
Both the guards sat their horses and pointed downwards, talking excitely all the time even though the
distance prevented the words reaching the girl. Keeping
back under the bank, Calamity watched the two men
until the driver joined them. After holding a conference,
one of the men helped the driver to mount behind him
and then they rode back in the direction from which
they came.

"Most likely figure I'm dead," she mused. "Poor old
Mark, I hope he doesn't hear about it."

Giving the men time to return, without them doing
so, Calamity considered the situation. Afoot, with a fair
number of miles to cover, she still must reach Robertstown. Most of the way was across range country, *cattle*
country. A long-horn range critter, be it cow, bull or
steer, feared human beings only when they came
mounted on a horse. Meeting cattle while afoot could
prove mighty dangerous. Even her whip might be inadequate protection if she walked into a longhorn's path.
Not that she aimed to discard the whip, it being her only
weapon. However she could not swim with it trailing
down; and swimming looked like the best way to start
her journey. Somewhere downstream the trail she had
been on must come down and cross the river. By reaching the fording place, Calamity could be sure of finding

a well-marked trail to Robertstown and on such might
be fortunate enough to meet travelers to give her protection.

Shoving herself forward from beneath the overhang,
Calamity felt the tug of the main current. A strong
swimmer, she found no difficulty in controlling herself
and decided to stay in the water as long as possible. On
land she might run across dangerous wild or domestic
animals, but not in the water.

To conserve her strength, Calamity concentrated on
staying afloat and allowed the current to carry her
along. She used her arms and legs as little as possible
and scanned the shore-line for the ford. Half a mile
below the point where the wagon crashed in, she had
seen no sign of the trail coming down. Not far ahead the
banks levelled down on the range side, but rose in a
steep slope across the river. Beyond that point the river
narrowed between two walls of rock and Calamity did
not need to hear the sound of rushing water to know
what the decrease in width meant. Already the current
increased its pace, tugging her on in the direction of the
rapids.

Striking out with arms and legs, Calamity aimed
herself in the direction of the range shore. The current
forced at her, but she struggled nearer and nearer to
land. Superbly fit, she still felt the tremendous strain
and could barely move her arms. Then her fingers
touched gravel as they dug into the water to draw her
forward. Another stroke and again she felt the bottom
of the river. Gathering all her remaining strength,
Calamity dragged herself on, lowering her feet to the
bottom and rising unsteadily. Three steps took her
ashore and she staggered on a short distance before col-
lapsing on to the hard, but so lovely and firm shingle of
the bank.

At last she felt rested sufficiently to rise. On climbing
to her feet, the first thing she thought about was her

whip. It still hung about her neck and she freed it. The care Calamity had lavished on the whip paid off at that moment. After a vigorous shaking, she held a serviceable tool—or weapon—in her hand. Overhead the sun shone down with enough power for her to dispense with stripping and wringing water from her clothes. Calamity had been soaked to the skin often enough not to worry unduly about it upon a warm day.

Standing for a moment, she studied her surroundings. The point where she came ashore appeared to be a valley bottom, a run-off for water gathered on the rolling range. By going to its top she could find a high point, get her bearings and start walking to Robertstown.

"Which same, I hate walking," she moaned, coiling the whip.

Unfortunately Calamity could see no alternative to walking, the rapids in the gorge prevented her from making further use of the river. So she started to walk along the valley floor, making for its upper end. Before she had gone fifty yards, a movement caught the corner of her eye. Alert for trouble, she turned and saw what looked like an enormous cougar crouching alongside a rock not more than twenty feet away.

Or was it a cougar?

While the color appeared to be the right tawny shade, the animal showed considerably more heft than any mountain lion Calamity had seen. The head also looked wrong. And, in the final analysis, that critter did not act like any cougar even to cross Calamity's path. Faced by a human being, the normal run of cougar would have only one aim in life, to put as much distance as possible between them. Unless Calamity guessed wrong, that damned critter had been stalking her and meant to attack.

Almost of its own volition the whip slid into her hand, its long lash shaking loose. Even as the animal started to rise, Calamity struck. Up and out coiled the whip, cracking savagely in the air. Much to her surprise, the animal sank down again but gave voice to a hideous roar. The sound came as a surprise, being unlike anything produced by a cougar's vocal chords, shocked Calamity into immobility and only one thing saved her from meeting the fate of old Gaff and a full-grown bull elk.

In the circus, the lioness learned to associate the sound of a whip crack with pain. Many times such a noise ended her intention to attack the puny man-thing which forced her to obey its will. So, although showing her rage in a roar, she did not press home her intended attack.

That momentary reprieve gave Calamity time to shake off the numb shock. If she was to die, then she aimed to make a fight of it. Back and forward lashed the whip, cracking explosively and as rapidly as she could make it. Roar after roar answered her and the lioness still crouched. Suddenly it steeled itself. Since escaping, it had killed and found the heady joy of tearing at warm, quivering flesh. Even before that, at the Mission, the lioness helped pull down prey, including human beings, and doing the latter caused its fear of man to ebb away. The old association of the whip died and the lioness gathered herself for a charge.

Calamity sensed the danger and knew what the animal meant to do. Nothing her whip could do would save her. Here it came! She saw the lioness—although still thinking of it as a strange variety of cougar—begin to move. A dull "whomp!" sounded and the lioness arched her back in sudden pain, bounded into the air, squawled and crashed down again to churn the air with flailing paws. Only faintly did Calamity hear the bark of a heavy calibre rifle. Her attention stayed on the thrashing body of the lioness, realizing what the small hole in the right rump meant when taken with the enormouse hole torn outwards at the left shoulder.

Kneeling at the top of the valley, Dusty Fog fed another bullet into the Sharps' breech and let out a sigh of relief. While he recognised the lioness' roar and expected to see a member of the species *Felis Leo*, he never thought to find its victim to be Calamity Jane. Sure he had heard the whip's cracks, but did not tie the sound in with that particular member of the bull whip breed.

Seeing Calamity handed Dusty a fair-sized shock, but he had not the time to wonder at the smallness of the world. The lioness looked to be ready for a charge and Dusty did not want to take chances on fancy shooting with a strange rifle, not when Calamity's life was at stake. Dropping to one knee, he sighted at the only target available. Such had been the power of the Sharps, that it drove its bullet the length of the lioness' body, destroying vital organs, before bursting out at the front end.

"Whooee!" the Kid breathed, lowering his Winchester unfired. "Now I know why old Gaff and that elk went under."

"Sure," Dusty replied, rising to his feet. "Way I heard it, a lion roars when charging so that it scares its prey into standing still for long enough to let it arrive."

"Lion?" said the Kid. "I thought they had all hair on their shoulders."

"That's a lioness—and what it's doing out here I'll never know."

"Come to that," drawled the Kid. "What's Calam doing here?"

By the time Dusty and the Kid reached her, Calamity had regained something of her usual aplomb. The last thing she wanted them to do was find her acting all woman and weepy; she had done enough of that with Mark back at the Mission.

"We meet you in the damnedest places, Calam," Dusty said, after ensuring that they need have no fear of the lioness.

"I've never been more pleased to see you pair," the girl answered, wondering how they would take the news that she deserted their *amigo* and made good her own escape. Wanting time to think, she went on, "That's the biggest cougar I've ever seen."

"It's fair-sized for a lioness too, I'd say," Dusty replied.

"Li—Lioness?" yelped Calamity. "You're joshing me. No, you're not. It must have come from that Mission."

"How long have you been afoot and in the sun, Calam gal?" inquired the Kid.

"What were you doing in the Mission, Calam?" Dusty put in before she could make her spluttering answer.

"Lying locked in a cellar most of the time," she replied. "They got Mark, Dusty."

"Who're they?" growled the Kid, sounding meaner than a razorback hog stropping its tusks on a fence rail.

"And how'd they get him?" Dusty went on.

"That bunch at the Mission're holding him prisoner." Calamity told the two Texans. "He got me out of there early on this morning."

"Where's Mark now?" demanded the Kid; face a cold Dog Soldier's mask.

Knowing the close bonds which existed between the members of the floating outfit, Calamity hesitated before making her reply.

"He got me out of the cellar where they'd held me, put me in the possum belly of the wagon and sent me out. I wanted to stay on with him, Dusty, Lon. I didn't want to leave him——."

"We know that, Calam gal," said the Kid gently. "Mark likely acted for the best—and so did you."

"Tell us all about it, Calam," Dusty ordered.

Before starting, Calam went to sit down on a rock.

The two Texans gathered before her and she started to give them the full story, beginning with meeting the Countess. Desperately she tried to remember details and keep everything in its correct sequence. Mark's life depended on her making no mistakes. On hearing of the Count's purpose at the Mission, Dusty interrupted the girl.

"So he's hard-rock mining there. That must take more men than we heard he had along."

"You know about him?" asked Calamity.

"Only that he moved into the Mission. Go on with your side of it."

Calamity continued talking, telling Dusty everything Mark instructed her to pass on. When she mentioned the guards Dusty and the Kid exchanged glances. At last the girl finished talking and looked at the small Texan expectantly.

"Four guards, two on either side of the trail though," the Kid remarked. "That makes it tricky. I could likely do it come dark, though."

"They've more at the main house and only one way in," warned Calamity. "You have to cross a fair piece of open ground that's lit with lamps."

"Those lions close off the rest of the building," Dusty agreed. "And one wrong move will see Mark dead."

Not one of the trio wanted to think that Mark might already be dead. Dusty knew Mark well enough to believe the blond giant felt reasonably safe. If the folk at the Mission believed Mark to be drugged and asleep, they could not connect him with the girl's escape. If they took the trouble to kidnap Mark and treated him differently to Calamity they must have a special use for him and would only kill him as a last resource. Bearing that in mind, Dusty made a decision, one of the hardest it had ever fallen on him to reach.

"Let's go," he said.

"To the Mission?" drawled the Kid in more of a statement than a question.

"Back to town."

Calamity and the Kid stared at Dusty in disbelief. While an angry comment welled up from Calamity, the Kid waited to be told why Dusty gave such an order. Silencing the girl, Dusty explained his reasons and Calamity grudgingly admitted that he called the play right.

"Garve Green can help, too," Dusty finished. "You're sure those jaspers aren't still after you, Calam?"

"Nope. They stopped on top of the cliff long enough to make sure I didn't show. Then they headed back to the Mission. 'Least that's where I figure they went. Happen they'd come along that trail over the river, theyd've seen me and I'd know about it."

"They were coming to town for supplies," Dusty remarked half to himself.

"So Mark told me," Calamity answered. "He allowed they had to fetch some in a hurry. Most likely they've gone back for the other wagon."

"They have another wagon?" asked Dusty and the other two could read interest in his soft-spoken words.

"Sure have," agreed the girl. "Way they lose 'em, it sure surprises me."

"Let's head for town," Dusty ordered.

"What's on your tricky Rio Hondo mind, Dusty?" demanded Calamity.

"I'll tell you after I've seen Garve Green," he replied and led the way up the slope.

Shortly before the trio reached Robertstown, they saw a small group of men heading in their direction. From the sight of four big bluetick hounds accompanying the men, Dusty concluded that they must be coming to meet him. The Kid needed no such conjecture, he already knew all but one member of the approaching group.

"It's Garve, Joe Vasquez, Vivian and Brinded, along of another rancher," he announced.

Coming up, Green's party halted alongside Dusty's group and showed surprise at seeing a girl seated behind the small Texan on his paint.

"We ran it down," Dusty told the newcomers on being questioned about the "cougar". To save time and explanation he did not mention the true nature of the animal. "I'm sorry we fetched you out for nothing, Major."

While a keen follower of hunting hounds, Major Calverly showed no disappointment. "From what I've been hearing, I wasn't keen on my hounds tangling with it," he answered.

"We may as well head back to town," Green commented. "The burying's this afternoon."

"Say, did you bring in that cougar's hide?" Vasquez inquired as the horses turned towards Robertstown.

"The bullet ripped it pretty bad," Dusty replied. "And we wanted to get Calamity to town."

"Which same none of us want to sound nosy——," hinted Green.

"My hoss fell fording the Wapiti," Calamity lied. "I started to walk and met up with Dusty and Lon along the trail."

"This's Calamity Jane," Dusty put in before any of the local men started to wonder about the meeting.

All Green's party showed considerable interest in Calamity; partly because everyone enjoys meeting a famous person, but also due to the fact that she dressed in a mighty unconventional manner and had a figure worth studying. Calamity's presence prevented too much interest being taken in the hunting and killing of the lioness, for which Dusty felt grateful.

"Say, Lon," Brinded remarked as they approached

the town. "Bratley and Laslo came bitching to me about how rough you handled them last night."

"You tell them from me they were lucky," the Kid answered. "If I'd been using my own rifle instead of Garvie's I'd not chanced busting the butt on them. I'd have used a bullet."

"I'll tell them," grinned the rancher.

On arrival in the town, Green looked at the ranchers. "Will you all be staying for the funeral?"

"Sure," Brinded replied.

"And me," Calamity went on. "Poor old Gaff, he made a hand."

Probably the old timer would have wished for no finer epitaph than those few words.

Watching the ranchers, Dusty could see no signs of the hostility and suspicion apparent the previous night. He knew that he could rely on them to give him full support for his plan. First, however, he had to obtain official approval for the plan.

"I'd like to have a word with you down to your office, Garve," Dusty said.

CHAPTER FIFTEEN

I'll Cut His Head Clean Off His Shoulders

Deftly coiling the length of thin wire around the piece of cheese, Happy Fileder pulled on the wooden handles and sliced a portion off. Calamity Jane gave a shudder as she watched the storekeeper at work.

"What's up, Calam, catch cold?" asked the Ysabel Kid.

"Nope," she replied. "Watching Happy there reminded me of the New Orleans Strangler. If he'd been using wire instead of a rope, I'd not be here now."

"I never did hear the full story about that," the Kid said.

"Maybe I'll tell you about it later," promised Calamity, thinking back to how she acted as a decoy to bring into the open a man who strangled eight girls in New Orleans.* "Right now I have to go see how Mrs. Happy's doing with that jacket I bought."

From the moment of their arrival in Robertstown, Dusty, the Kid and Calamity had been busy. While Calamity went to the store and attended to her boss' business, buying a jacket at the same time, Dusty and the Kid interviewed the town marshal, telling Green of

*Told in THE BULL WHIP BREED by J. T. Edson.

Mark's predicament and receiving a promise of every possible assistance. Guessing that Dusty aimed to make a move that night, Calamity decided she would need a coat—her own being with her saddle at the Mission—and visited Happy's store. The only available coat proved a shade too large, but Happy's wife offered to alter it and Calamity had come to try it on.

At that moment Dusty entered the store. The Kid looked expectantly and asked, "How's everything?"

"The last telegraph message just came in. It told us all we need to know."

During the ride back to town, Dusty had given the matter of Mark's kidnapping serious thought. To check on his theories, he sent telegraph messages to the four nearest towns' marshals and requested information. Certain significant points came to light. The Count bought supplies in two of the towns, alternating between them and Robertstown so that nobody would suspect the number of men actually at the Mission. One commodity he did not buy in the other towns was meat, although he did so from Robertstown. Dusty understood the point of that. Slow-elking would be safer, done carefully, than trying to steal other types of food. To avoid suspicion, the Count purchased some meat in town. To prove Dusty's theory, neither of the other towns has been troubled by slow-elkers.

With that problem settled, Dusty gave his attention to the more important business of rescuing his *amigo*. He learned all he could about the Mission and knew that only careful organisation, skilled work and a fair amount of luck would free Mark. If anything went wrong, they were not likely to find Mark alive when finally forcing an entrance to the building.

"It's going to be the way you planned?" Calamity asked.

"That's how it'll have to be," agreed Dusty.

"I'll go see about the coat then," the girl said and walked into the rear room where Happy's wife waited.

"The men'll gather just after dark, Lon," Dusty said after the girl left. "It won't be easy."

"It'll be hard as hell," admitted the Kid.

Happy strolled over from where he had been doing some work and nodded to the two Texans. So far only the marshal, deputy and three ranchers knew of the kidnapping and the storekeeper started to talk about old Gaff's death. A wagon halted outside the store and Happy directed a glance towards it.

"Hello," he said. "They're early this time."

"Who?" asked Dusty, seeing two riders dismount and join the man who jumped from the wagon's box.

"Some of the men from the Mission. I thought it'd be a week at least afore they came in again."

While Dusty had hoped for such a break, he never expected it to come off. Unfortunately there would be no time to prepare the Kid for what Dusty planned to do. However the small Texan figured he could rely on his *amigo* to act right even without instructions.

"Lon!" he said.

Only one word, but it warned the Kid that something unexpected had turned up. In fact the Kid had already seen the possibilities offered by the wagon's arrival. Although his thought did not run parallel with Dusty's he guessed what the other had in mind.

Neither Texan showed any sign, apart from the one glance out of the window, of being interested in the newcomers. Standing with their backs to the door, elbow on the counter, they ignored the sound of the door opening. On entering the room, the three Italians saw nothing to worry them and started to walk towards the counter. Dusty wanted the men right up before he made his move and listened to the sound of their feet drawing closer. Three more steps, four at most, ought to put them just where he wanted them.

Suddenly the steps halted and he heard startled exclamations, at the same time he saw the one thing that could spoil all his plans.

To be fair to Calamity, she could not be expected to know about the arrival of the three Italians. Certainly she would not have strolled so casually out of the backroom had she been aware of their presence. Just two seconds too late, she realised the position.

Despite the shock of seeing a girl they believed to be dead, the two guards acted with commendable speed. Fetching his rifle from the crook of his arm, the man at the right found himself with a problem; knowing who of the people before him he should shoot at first. His revolver-armed companion grabbed for the weapon, but the driver carried only a knife.

Dusty and the Kid both went into action after their favorite fashion and Happy took a hurried dive behind the counter. Showing an equal grasp of the situation, Calamity thrust herself backwards to cannon into Happy's wife and shove her into the safety of the other room.

Even as he turned, left hand driving across to draw the right side Colt, Dusty studied and assessed the situation. While the rifleman might be the furthest of the trio, he offered the greatest danger. Uncertain of who to take, the man with the rifle wavered for an instant. When dealing with the Rio Hondo gun wizard, such a delay could only prove fatal. Flame lashed from the Colt's barrel and lead tore into the man's chest, knocking him staggering and causing him to drop the rifle.

Although the Kid followed his usual procedure of carrying his Winchester, it rested some feet away on the counter. Springing forward, he caught up the rifle with his right hand curling into position around the butt. His summing up of the matter led him to Dusty's conclusion and so he pivoted around knowing what to do. One glance told him the second man's potentiality and ability. Throwing the rifle to his shoulder, the Kid aimed and drove a bullet through the man's leg before the revolver came clear of its holster.

Whirling around, the driver made a dash for the front door. Dusty holstered his Colt and leapt after the man, yelling, "Don't shoot him, Lon!"

Before the driver could open the door, Dusty reached him. Shooting out his hand, Dusty caught the man by the collar and heaved him back into the room. Steel glinted as the man whipped out his knife. Crouching slightly on bent knees, the man held his knife close in to his body, with left hand out in front as an aid to balance.

Seeing how the man stood, the Kid knew him to be better than fair with a knife for the posture guarded the vital areas of the belly and throat against another knife. It would also defeat the efforts of most unarmed defense measures. Swinging his rifle on to the counter once more, the Kid started to pull his bowie knife from its sheath.

"I'll take him, Dusty!" he yelled.

"Stay out of it," Dusty answered. "I want him alive and unharmed."

Dusty had learned enough about knife-fighting from the Kid to know the risks he took. Out in the center of the store he had room to move around, which was one of the factors that helped him reach his decision. Under more cramped conditions he would not have attempted to capture the man with his bare hands.

Advancing with a cautious shuffle step, the driver made short stabs and passes in Dusty's direction. Suddenly the knife flashed from his right to the left hand and he lunged in, driving it at Dusty's belly. Alert for any eventuality, Dusty had been watching the knife and saw his danger. Quickly the small Texan pivoted his body backwards on his right foot, avoiding the lunge. Up whipped Dusty's right arm, striking the driver's extended left from underneath. Then Dusty caught the man's wrist in his left hand to drag him forward and off balance. Up came Dusty's right arm, curling over and around the trapped limb at the bicep. A grunt of agony left the Italian's lips as Dusty bent the arm against the joint. Before he could make a move to escape, Dusty gave a heave on the arm which caused him to drop the knife, then hooked his left leg upwards with a foot and brought him crashing to the floor.

After kicking the knife away, Dusty drew his right-hand Colt and pressed it against the man's head. An instant later the Kid arrived, his bowie knife adding to the menace which effectively ended any attempts at resistance. Bending down Dusty laid hold of the man with his left hand and hauled him to his feet. Deprived of his knife, the driver gave up the struggle and stared in a scared manner from his captors to Calamity as she emerged from the backroom.

"Will somebody tell me what the hell's come off?" demanded Happy, rising from behind the counter.

Ignoring the question, Dusty snapped an order which sent the Kid darting from the store. Several people ran towards the building, including Marshal Green, but the Kid could see no sign of departing riders which would tell that more members of the Mission party had been outside.

"What's all the ruckus?" Green asked as he came up.

"We just nailed three of the Mission bunch," the Kid replied.

Green entered the store, glanced at the two wounded men and then joined Dusty at the counter.

"We've got our way into the Mission," the small Texan told him.

"You mean inside that wagon?"

"Sure."

"It won't work, Dusty. We can't get there before dawn and in daylight the guard'll know right off it's not their man on the box."

"Their man's going to be on it," Dusty said.

For a moment the full import of Dusty's words did not strike the marshal. Then the light came and Green saw difficulties.

"He'll never do it, Dusty," the marshal stated.

"He'll do it," Dusty answered in a quiet, but deadly earnest voice. "Calam, you and Lon see to those other two."

"Yo!" replied the girl and went to obey.

"Do you speak English?" Dusty asked, turning back to the driver.

"*Io non capisco*," replied the man.

"Says he don't understand, Cap'n," Happy put in. "He knows some, but it don't matter. I lived among Eye-talians for years back East and speak their lingo."

"Tell him I know about the man they're holding at the Mission," Dusty instructed, hiding his delight at the good fortune of finding an interpreter. "Make sure that he knows Mark Counter's a real good friend. Then tell him he's taking us into the valley in his wagon."

Without wasting time in asking questions, Happy thought out the necessary words and listened to the spat-out reply.

"He says he won't do it, Cap'n," Happy reported. "Allows he's a *Mafiosi*, that's a member of a secret society among the Eye-talians, and he'll die before he betrays their oath."

Studying the man, Dusty wondered how he might bring about a change of mind. Mere physical pain would not do it, even if they did not require the man in fit shape to handle the wagon. So Dusty must find some other way. Fortunately he had some experience in the matter. On two occasions during the War Between The States Dusty went on missions with the Confederate spy Belle Boyd.* From her, he learned much about the ways of bending an unwilling prisoner to one's will. Among other things, Belle explained the kind of tactics most likely to influence men of different racial types. Thinking back to her advice, Dusty tried to decide on the best way to handle a Latin.

To hide his uncertainty, Dusty assumed an assured air and reached nonchalantly towards the counter. He meant to take a piece of cheese and eat it, to make the Italian believe he did not doubt that he would have his way, but his hand froze in mid air. Looking down at the wire cheese-cutter, Dusty remembered. Calamity's words—overheard as he approached and entered the store—about the New Orleans Strangler.

"How strong's that wire, Happy?" he asked.

The question came as something of a surprise, but the storekeeper shrugged and replied, "As strong as you can get, Cap'n. It's out of a bust piano."

"Loan me it, please. And sell me that ham you're sending to the hotel."

"The ha——," began Happy, but saw the serious lines on Dusty's face. "Sure thing, Cap'n. I'll fetch it for you."

Happy's puzzled expression did not change when, on returning with the ham, Dusty asked him to hold it upright. Watched by the Italian—plus a bug-eyed storekeeper and marshal—Dusty looped the wire around the wide base of the ham and began to pull on the handles. At first Dusty wondered if the wire would stand the strain. If it broke, he would have to find some other way of dealing with the man. Slowly the wire cut into the

---

*Told in THE COLT AND THE SABRE.

ham, sinking deeper and deeper until reaching the bone. Pulling the ham from Happy's hands, the small Texan held it suspended from the wire and showed it to the Italian.

"Tell him that's he's going to drive us into the Valley. I'll be standing right behind him, with the wire around his neck. The first time he makes a wrong move, I'll cut his head clean off his shoulders."

Without making it obvious, Dusty watched the man as Happy translated his threat. Fear glowed momentarily in the man's eyes and his hand made an involuntary movement towards his throat. Dusty felt a touch of satisfaction. Once more it appeared that Belle Boyd had given wise advice. To the Latin temperament, the threat of the wire worked where neither physical abuse or a bullet would. Already the man's imagination pictured what that noose of wire could to do him and his eyes never left the dangling ham.

"Reckon he'll do it, Dusty?" asked Green.

"I reckon he will. Take him to the jail, Garve. And leave that ham hanging where he can see it."

"It's your play."

"I'll come along," Dusty remarked. "We've plenty to do before it's time to make a start."

The local doctor had arrived and relieved Calamity of her work. Joining the Texans and Green, she left the store and walked along to the jail. Once there, Dusty passed orders for the posse to be gathered and escorted the driver into the building.

If attention to detail could command success, Green mused, as he watched the small Texan make arrangements with the posse, Mark Counter was as good as released.

Patiently Dusty told the assembled men of his suspicions and the kidnapping of his *amigo*. A low rumble passed among the cowhands present as they heard that the people at the Mission might be responsible for the slow-elking, which also tied in with the missing ranch hands. However Dusty warned them that he had no proof of guilt and that they went to the Mission mainly to rescue Mark. Nobody questioned the small Texan's right to give orders. Watching the men, Green felt relief as he saw the dying away of the suspicion with which different ranch crews previously studied each other. It seemed that most folks in Roberts County only wanted an excuse to return to the old friendly ways of before the slow-elking.

After assigning each man his task and making sure he knew it, Dusty explained his plan. Calamity, the Kid, Happy and Dusty would be in the wagon with seven more men. Making sure that they did not come into sight of the guards at the valley's mouth, Green and the remainder were to follow on horses. When the rear party heard shooting, they must charge in and launch an attack while the guards concentrated on the wagon's occupants. If the scheme failed, they would press home their attack and take the Mission by force.

"I want a few sticks of dynamite fused up ready in the wagon," Dusty remarked. "If they get inside, we'll have something to open the doors."

"I'll tend to it," Happy promised.

"How about a fresh team for the wagon, Dusty?" Calamity, as driver until approaching the entrance to the valley, asked.

"Do they usually make a change here?" he inquired.

"Nope," Green supplied.

"Then we don't take the chance. It'll mean tuckered-out horses, but we won't need them fresh and frisky if everything goes all right."

"Them guards are going to ask where their pards are," the Kid commented.

It seemed that Dusty had already thought of that contingency. "Happy'll tell that jasper what to say."

"I sure hope you tell *me* what to say," drawled the storekeeper.

"If they ask, he's to tell them that his pards thought they saw Calamity and stayed back to have a close look," Dusty explained.

"Will those guards believe it?" asked the Kid.

"I don't know," Dusty admitted. "We'll have to hope they do."

"Will you be able to keep out of sight and still hold that jasper, Dusty?" Green wanted to know.

"We gave it a try. Calam sat on the box and we let the front of the cover down. If the feller sits in the middle of the box, I can hold him. Trouble is I can't see much through the slit that's all we can chance using."

"Can you manage with it?"

"I'll have to, Garve. It won't be too bad though, we can hear everything the driver says. Any more questions?"

As nobody could think of any point which had not been brought up, the meeting ended. There would be no time to waste and Dusty wanted to get started as soon as possible. Satisfied that he could do no more and had made every possible plan, he gave the order to mount up.

During the journey to the edge of the Wapiti Hills, the Kid rode ahead as scout. There was a chance that Count Giovanni did not accept his men's assurance of Calamity's death and sent a party out to search for proof. If so, Dusty did not want the posse seen and an alarm raised. He figured that the Kid's Comanche training ought to lick anything the Mission crowd put out and so could expect a warning long before they saw the posse.

Dawn found them following the trail through the Wapiti Hills and soon after the Kid returned to say the way was clear. He and Calamity entered the wagon and let down the rear canopy. Ordering the Italian driver to take Calamity's place on the box, Dusty adjusted the wire noose and then had the covers lowered.

"Tell him to start driving," Dusty ordered Happy and drew the wire taut.

He wondered if he would carry out his threat if it came to a push and could reach no conclusion. Not that it mattered as long as the driver believed him capable of doing so.

In the darkness of the wagon Calamity shut her eyes. "Lord," she whispered. "I've never been one for praying—but let everything go off right."

CHAPTER SIXTEEN

It Started a Run

Sweat poured down Mark Counter's face and soaked his bare torso as he stood with spraddled legs and every muscle straining against the pull of the two horses. The Count, Baton and all the Italians not on guard duty or with the supply wagon stood before the Mission building and watched the herculean struggle Mark put up. Running his tongue top across his lips, Baton wondered if he could bring the business to an end. While a professional killer, he did not approve of the way in which the Count brought death to those who antagonized him. However Baton knew he dare not intervene. His services might be needed, but the Count would not let that stand in his way if crossed.

"Make them pull harder!" yelled the Count.

The two men at the horses' heads heard and slashed at their charges with quirts. Behind each horse, a rope stretched to Mark's wrist, tied in such a manner that he could grip it in his hand. So far he had been able to keep his arms slightly bent, but the enormous strain was beginning to tell. Only one thing favored Mark in his struggle. Underfoot the earth had become packed to an iron-hard mass on which the horses found difficulty in obtaining a grip that allowed them to throw all their strength into the contest. Hooves churned, quirts lashed and nostrils gave out snorts as the horses flung their weight into the effort.

Excited comments left the lips of the watching men as Mark's arms straightened. Desperately he tried to draw the horse back if only a fraction and a low gasp of pain broke from him. Making bets, talking and staring at the blond giant, none of the party had eyes or attention for anything else.

As Dusty knew it would be, his range of vision was limited to the Italian driver's back. He heard one of the guards call out and gave a gentle tug on the wire. Not enough to panic the man into an involuntary gesture, but sufficient to act as a reminder of the fate awaiting him.

"He's saying what you told him!" Happy breathed as the driver spoke.

Then the wagon rolled on once more. Still Dusty could see nothing, but gauged the distance they had traveled. He heard the excited shouts and other sounds ahead, drawing closer by the second, and decided to take a chance on looking out.

Drawing aside the canopy slightly with his left hand, Dusty saw some of the men standing before the main building and wondered what held their interest. Carefully he eased the canopy further, passing the handles of the wire to Happy, and saw Mark. Sudden rage roared through Dusty at the sight and a low snarl left the Kid's lips.

"Not yet!" Dusty growled, his voice brittle with the effort of holding down his own feelings. "Wait until we're up closer."

Obscenities poured from the Kid's lips and by his side Calamity stirred restlessly, fingering the carbine Dusty loaned her. Closer rolled the wagon and Dusty's fists clenched so hard that they hurt. Slowly his hands went to the canopy. When making his plans, Dusty decided that a quick method of clearing the exits was required. He caused the upper edges of the canopy to be cut so that only the smallest possible piece held them in place. A quick jerk on either side broke the last remaining pieces and the covers fell aside.

"Now!" he barked and lunged through the open front on to the wagon box.

Baton saw the small Texan appear and the other men in the wagon. Reaching for his gun, he opened his mouth to warn the men about him that the valley's defenses had been breached.

From the wagon's box, Dusty sprang forward. One foot landed on the rump of the right side horse and he dived from it. Even while in the air, his hands crossed and the matched Colts came into them. Landing on straddled legs, Dusty missed death by inches as Baton cut loose on him. Flame ripped from the right-hand Colt and the gun-hand jerked backwards as if struck by an unseen force. On the heels of the first shot he fired, Dusty slammed lead with his left-hand weapon at one of the Italians who showed signs of recovering rapidly from the shock of his appearance.

Following on Dusty's heels, the Kid landed alongside the small Texan and his rifle cracked. Struck by a bullet, the rope attached to Mark's right wrist split and snapped. Blurring the lever, the Kid ejected an empty case and fed a loaded bullet into the breech, changing his point of aim in between. Born with the Comanche's love of horses, the Kid could not bring himself to kill the animal at Mark's right, yet he knew he must act fast. Freed of the counter-pull the right-side horse lunged forward and dragged the blond giant after it. Sighting carefully, the Kid fired. His bullet ripped through the muscular part of the neck just over the vertebrae, di-

rected there because, aimed correctly, it would drop the
horse instantly unconscious to recover a few minutes
later. If the bullet went a shade low, it stood a chance of
breaking the spine and causing just as immediate, if
more permanent, collapse. From the way the horse went
down, the Kid figured he had creased and not killed it.

Startled by the shooting and Dusty's departure, the
wagon's team showed signs of spooking. Happy
reached out, caught the driver by the shoulders and
hauled him backwards into the wagon. At the same moment Calamity grabbed the reins in her left hand and
stepped on to the box. Ignoring the shots and noise
made by the remainder of the party leaving the wagon,
she gained control of the horses and swung them away
from the action.

On jerking the driver back, Happy made use of
another piece of Dusty's planning. Before leaving town,
a set of handcuffs had been fastened to the central
canopy support with one cuff trailing open ready. One
of the men clamped the cuff on to the driver's wrist.
Fastened in such a manner he could make no trouble
and did not require watching. With that duty attended
to, Happy flung himself from the wagon.

Deftly swinging the wagon clear, Calamity booted on
its brake. She let the reins fall, scooped up the carbine
and threw a shot at one of the men who had been controlling the horses used to torture Mark, stopping him
as he drew a knife with the intention of attacking the
blond giant.

Only a few of the Count's men carried weapons and
not one of them found time to do more than make a
token resistance. Half of the wagon's party, armed with
rifles, darted back in the direction they had come and
sporadic shots passed between them and the entrance
guards. While the guards' positions offered protection
from an attack at the valley's mouth, they proved inade-

quate against shots coming from the direction of the house. One guard went down dead, a second caught a bullet in the arm and the other pair heard the thunder of approaching hooves as Marshal Green brought up the remainder of the posse. That ended resistance from the two, they threw aside their rifles and surrendered.

During the confusion which ensued after Dusty's appearance, the Count turned and darted back into the Mission, closing its door behind him. He saw the danger and went hurriedly in the direction of the mine shaft to gather reinforcements.

Calamity bounded from the wagon and raced towards Mark. Already the remainder of the Count's bodyguard saw the futility of resistance and discarded their weapons or raised their arms. Leaving the Italians to Happy and the others, Dusty and the Kid ran forward, reaching Mark at the same time that Calamity arrived. On his hands and knees, the blond giant looked up at his friends. His breath came in long, ragged gasps and his chest heaved as he sucked in air.

"How is it, Mark?" asked Dusty.

Slowly Mark flexed his left arm, then he managed a grin. "I'll live."

"You're not hurt bad, are you?" Calamity inquired.

"Nothing that loving care won't cure, Calam gal," Mark assured her.

"Where's that Count, or whatever they call him?" growled the Kid.

"I saw a fat jasper run back into the house," Calamity replied.

"Let's go get him," Dusty said gently, that deadly gentleness which the others knew so well.

"Loan me a gun, Dusty," Mark suggested, levering himself to his feet. "I want to settle with him myself."

Passing over his left-hand Colt, Dusty led the others up to the main doors of the building. Keeping to one side of it, he gripped the handle, turned and tried to open it.

"Fastened," he said and raised his voice in a yell, "Happy, bring the dynamite up here."

"Yo!" the storekeeper replied and went to obey.

A distant rumbling, like thunder yet seeming to come from underground in the building, reached the Texans' ears as they waited for the arrival of the explosives. Placing the bundle into position, Dusty motioned the others back and lit the fuse. He walked off to a safe distance and waited until the dynamite exploded. The door burst inwards as the explosion roared out and the three Texans charged in with their guns ready.

"Where's the Countess?" demanded Calamity as she followed on Mark's heels.

"Dead," he replied. "The lions got her. We're going to shoot them when we're done, to get the bodies out, Dusty."

Before Dusty could question the statement, several half-dressed girls came running from the rear of the building and Whales followed, dirt and dust covering him. He skidded to a halt, staring at the strange faces.

"Where is he?" Mark growled, moving forward.

"Down in the tunnel," Whales replied. "He came rushing down, shouting and hollering like he was crazy. Rushed into me and knocked me over damned near. I fell against the shoring——It wasn't safe, I'd kept telling him it wasn't——."

"What happened?" Dusty snapped.

"It started a run. The whole damned tunnel system's caved in."

Thrusting by the man, Dusty, Mark, the Kid and Calamity went into the rear of the building. Mark led the way to the mine tunnel, but one glance told them all they needed to know. Where the tunnel had been, only a mass of fallen rock remained.

"We'll have to try to get them out," Dusty said,

realising that some of the men must be underneath.

"Sure," Mark agreed. "But there's not much hope. From what I saw while I was down there, once a run started, the whole damned lot'd go."

"What a way to go," Dusty said as he turned to go and start organising the rescue attempt.

"It's a lousy way to go," Mark agreed. "I wouldn't have wished it even on him. Well, he wanted gold, now he's down among it—and he'll likely stay there."